Romantic Getaways

Escape to Paradise!

This Valentine's Day, escape to four of the world's most romantic destinations with these sparkling books from Harlequin Romance!

From the awe-inspiring desert to vibrant Barcelona, from the stunning coral reefs of Australia to heart-stoppingly romantic Venice, get swept away by these wonderful romances!

The Sheikh's Convenient Princess
by Liz Fielding

The Unforgettable Spanish Tycoon
by Christy McKellen

The Billionaire of Coral Bay
by Nikki Logan

Her First-Date Honeymoon
by Katrina Cudmore

Dear Reader,

When my editor asked if I'd consider writing another "sheikh" book, I had one of those tingly "yes!" moments. From that day in 1919 when Edith Maude Hull sent women's hearts aflutter with the publication of *The Sheik*, he has been the ultimate fantasy figure. Distant, enigmatic, powerful...

Ibrahim al-Ansari, disinherited, alone in his fortress home, is all of those things. It takes Ruby Dance, crème de la crème of temporary personal assistants—and a woman with a closet full of skeletons—to unlock the secret Bram has been hiding and reveal the hero within.

Let him lift you before him onto the saddle of Antares and, safe in his strong arms, sweep you away!

With love,

Liz

The Sheikh's Convenient Princess

Liz Fielding

HARLEQUIN® ROMANCE

Recycling programs for this product may not exist in your area.

ISBN-13: 978-0-373-74420-6

The Sheikh's Convenient Princess

First North American Publication 2017

This edition published by arrangement with Harlequin Books S.A.

For questions and comments about the quality of this book, please contact us at CustomerService@Harlequin.com.

Printed in U.S.A.

Liz Fielding was born with itchy feet. She made it to Zambia before her twenty-first birthday and, gathering her own special hero and a couple of children on the way, lived in Botswana, Kenya and Bahrain—with pauses for sightseeing pretty much everywhere in between. She now lives in the west of England, close to the Regency grandeur of Bath and the ancient mystery of Stonehenge, and these days lets her pen do the traveling.

For news of upcoming books visit Liz's website at lizfielding.com.

Books by Liz Fielding

Harlequin Romance

Flirting with Italian
The Last Woman He'd Ever Date
Vettori's Damsel in Distress

Harlequin KISS

Anything but Vanilla...
For His Eyes Only

Visit the Author Profile page
at Harlequin.com for more titles.

I'm dedicating this, my 65th title, to my wonderful readers, some of whom have been with me from the first Friday in December 1992 when my first book—*An Image of You*—was published. You are my inspiration.

CHAPTER ONE

'BRAM...'

Bram Ansari had answered the phone without looking up from a document that had just arrived by courier. 'Hamad...I was about to call you.'

'Then you've received the summons to Father's birthday *majlis*.'

'It arrived ten minutes ago. I imagine I have you to thank for that.'

'No. It's his wish. He's sick, Bram. It's a significant birthday. You need to be home.'

His brother did not sound particularly happy at the prospect.

'I doubt everyone thinks that.'

'It's covered. The old man has negotiated a secret deal with the Khadri family.'

'A deal?' Bram frowned. 'What kind of deal?' The last time he'd seen Ahmed Khadri the man had threatened to cut his throat if he ever stepped foot in Umm al Basr. 'Tell me.'

As his brother explained the secret deal his father had negotiated to enable Bram to return home the colour leached out of the day until the sky, the sea, the flowers overflowing the tower turned grey.

'No...'

'I'm sorry, Bram, but at least you're prepared.

If Bibi hadn't managed to smuggle a note to her sister you would have been presented with a *fait accompli*.'

'You think I can go through with this?'

'It's the price that must be paid.'

'But I won't be the one paying it!' He took a breath. 'How is your family?' he asked, cutting Hamad short when he would have argued. 'The new baby?'

'*In sh'Allah*, all my precious girls are thriving. Safia sends her fondest wishes and thanks for the gifts.' He hesitated. 'She said to say that you are always in her prayers.'

Bram ended the call then swept the invitation from the table in impotent fury. The longed-for chance to kneel at his father's feet and beg his forgiveness had come attached to a tangle of string that would take more than prayers to unravel. It would need a miracle.

The phone beeped, warning him that he had a missed call. He glanced at the screen and ignored it. His aide was spending a long weekend with friends in the Alps and the last thing he needed right now was a joyous description of the snow conditions.

Qa'lat al Mina'a, perched high on its rocky promontory, shimmered like a mirage in the soft pink haze of the setting sun.

Far below, beyond a perfect curve of white sand, a dhow was drifting slowly along the coast under a dark red sail and for a brief moment Ruby felt as if she might have been transported back into some *Arabian Nights* fantasy, flying in on a magic carpet rather than a gleaming black helicopter.

The illusion was swiftly shattered as they circled to land.

The fortress might appear, at first glance, to be a picturesque ruin, a reminder of a bygone age, but behind the mass of purple bougainvillaea billowing against its walls was a satellite dish, antennae—all the trappings of the communications age, powered by an impressive range of solar panels facing south where the *jebel* fell away to the desert.

And the tower did not stand alone. Below it she glimpsed courtyards, arches, gardens surrounding an extensive complex that spread down to the shore where a very twenty-first century gunmetal-grey military-style launch was sheltered in a harbour hewn from the rock. And they were descending to a purpose-built helipad. This was not some romantically crumbling stronghold out of a fantasy; the exterior might be battered by weather and time but it contained the headquarters of a very modern man.

As they touched down, a middle-aged man in a

grey robe and skullcap approached the helicopter at a crouching run. He opened the door, glanced at her with astonishment and then shouted something she couldn't hear to the pilot.

He returned a don't-ask-me shrug from his seat. Sensing a problem, Ruby didn't wait but unclipped her safety belt, swung open the door and jumped down.

'*As-salaam aleykum. Ismee*, Ruby Dance,' she said, raising her voice above the noise of the engine. 'Sheikh Ibrahim is expecting me.'

She didn't wait for a response but shouldered the neat satchel that contained everything she needed for work, nodded her thanks to the pilot and, leaving the man to follow with her wheelie suitcase, she crossed to steps that led down to the shelter of the courtyard below.

The air coming off the sea was soft and moist—bliss after hours cooped up in the dry air of even the most luxurious private jet—while below her were tantalising glimpses of terraces cut into the hill, each shaded by ancient walls and vine-covered pergolas. There was a glint of water running through rills and at her feet clove-scented dianthus and thyme billowed over onto the steps.

It was beautiful, exotic, unexpected. Not so far from the fantasy after all.

Behind her the pilot, keen to get home, was already winding up the engine and she lifted her head to watch the helicopter take off, bracing herself against buffeting from the down force of the blades. As it wheeled away back towards the capital of Ras al Kawi, leaving her cut off from the outside world, she half lifted a hand as if to snatch it back.

'*Madaam…*'

Despite her confident assertion that she was expected, it was clear that her arrival had come as a surprise but, before she could respond to the agitated man who was following her down the steps, a disembodied voice rang out from below, calling out something she did not understand.

Before she could move, think, the owner of the voice was at the foot of the steps, looking up at her, and she forgot to breathe.

Sheikh Ibrahim al-Ansari was no longer the golden prince, heir to the throne of Umm al Basr, society magazine cover favourite—a carefree young man with nothing on his mind but celebrating his sporting triumphs in some fashionable nightclub.

Disgraced, disinherited and exiled from his father's court when his arrest for a naked romp in a London fountain had made front page news, his face was harder, the bones more defined, the natural lines cut a little deeper. And not just lines. Running through the edge of his left brow, slicing through his cheekbone before disappearing into a short-clipped beard was a thin scar—the kind left by the slash of a razor-sharp knife—and dragging at the corner of his eye and his lip so that his face was not quite in balance. The effect was brutal, chilling, mesmerising.

He was never going to be the beast—his bone structure beneath the silky golden skin was too perfect, the tawny eyes commanding and holding all her attention, but he was no longer the beautiful young man who had appeared in society magazines alongside European aristocrats, millionaires, princes. Whose photograph, trophy in hand, had regularly graced the covers of the glossier lifestyle magazines.

She was momentarily distracted by a flash of pink as a droplet of water, caught in the sun's dying rays, slid down one of the dark, wet curls that clung to his neck.

She was standing with her back to the setting sun and he raised a hand to shade his eyes. 'What the devil?'

Mouth dry, brain freewheeling and with no connection between them, her lips parted but her breath stuck in her throat as a second drop of water joined the first, hung there until the force of gravity overcame it and it dropped to a wide shoulder, slid into the hollow of his collarbone.

She watched, mesmerised, as it spilled over, trickled down his broad chest, imagining how it would feel against her hand if she reached out to capture it.

The thought was so intense that she could feel the tickle of chest hair against her palm, the wet, sun-kissed skin, and instinctively closed her hand.

She hadn't expected him to be wearing a pin-striped suit or the formal flowing robes of a desert prince, but it was her first encounter with an employer wearing nothing but a towel—a man whose masculinity was underlined by the scars left by his chosen sports.

'Who are you?' he demanded.

Not some empty-headed ninny to stand there gawping at the kind of male body more usually seen in moody adverts for aftershave, that was for sure, and, sending an urgent message to her feet, she stepped down to his level.

'Not the devil, Sheikh.' She uncurled her clenched hand and offered it to him as she introduced herself. 'Ruby Dance. I've been sent by the Garland Agency to hold the fort while Peter Hammond recovers from his injuries.'

Sheikh Ibrahim stared at her hand for what felt like forever, then, ignoring it, he looked up.

'Injuries?' Dark brows were pulled down in a confused frown. 'What injuries?'

She lowered her hand. Well, that explained the confusion at her arrival. Obviously the message about his aide's accident had failed to reach him.

'I understand that Mr Hammond crashed off his snowboard early this morning,' she replied, putting his lapse of manners down to shock. 'I was told that he'd spoken to you.'

'Then you were misinformed,' he said. 'How bad is it?'

'The last I heard was that he'd been airlifted to hospital. I'll see if I can get an update.' She took her phone from her bag. 'Will I get a signal?' He didn't bother to answer but she got five strong bars—those antennae weren't just for show—and hit the first number on her contact list.

There were endless seconds of waiting for the international connection—endless seconds in which he continued to stare at her. It was the look of someone who was sure he'd seen her before but couldn't think where.

'Ruby? Is everything okay?' Amanda Garland, the founder of the Garland Agency, had called her first thing, asking her to drop whatever she was doing, fly out to Qa'lat al Mina'a and hold the fort until other arrangements could be made.

'Yes…'

'Tell me.' There was no fooling Amanda.

Ruby swallowed, took a breath. She was imagining it, she knew. It had been years since her photograph had been all over the media, but his sculptured chest, the smattering of hair arrowing down beneath the towel—far too reminiscent of that scene in the fountain—was wrecking her concentration.

In an attempt to get a grip, she turned away, focusing on the sea, the misted shape of the dhow far below, dropping its sails as it turned to edge up the creek.

'Ruby!'

'Everything's fine,' Ruby said quickly. 'The flight went without a hitch but my arrival has come as something of a surprise. It seems that Sheikh Ibrahim did not get the message about Peter's accident.'

'What?' Amanda was clearly shocked. 'I'm so sorry, Ruby. Is there anything I can do? Do you want me to speak to the Sheikh?'

'All I need is an update on Mr Hammond's condition.' Amanda gave her the details. 'And which hospital…? Thanks—that will be perfect. I'll speak to you later.' She disconnected.

'Well?' he demanded as she turned to him, keeping her gaze fixed on his face. Tawny eyes, a hawkish nose, a mouth with a one-sided tug that gave it a cruelly sensuous droop—

'Peter has broken his left leg in two places, torn a ligament in his wrist and cracked some ribs,' she said, blotting out the thoughts that had no place in a business environment—thoughts that she didn't want in her head. 'They've pinned him back together and he'll be flown home in a day or two. Amanda is going to text me contact details.'

'Who is Amanda?'

Hello, good to meet you and thank you for rushing to fill the gap would have been polite. *Thank you for putting my mind at rest* was pretty much a minimum in the circumstances. But Ruby had long ago learned to keep her expression neutral, to never show what she was thinking or feeling, and she focused on the question rather than his lack of manners.

'Amanda Garland.' The name would normally be enough but Sheikh Ibrahim did not work in London, where it was shorthand for the best in business and domestic staff. There was no smile of recognition, no gratitude for the fact that his injured aide's first thought had been to summon a replacement. 'The Garland Agency supplies temps, nannies and domestic staff to an international clientele. Amanda is also Peter's godmother.' She returned her phone to her bag and took out the heavy white envelope that she'd sent with the driver who'd picked her up. 'When he sent an SOS for someone to hold the fort, she called me. I have her letter of introduction.'

She'd already had her hand ignored once and did not make the mistake of offering it to him so that he could ignore the letter too, but waited for him to reach for it.

'A letter of introduction from someone I don't know?'

'Perhaps Mr Hammond thought you would trust his judgement.'

'How good would your judgement be if you were lying in the snow with a broken leg?' he demanded.

'Since that's never going to happen, I couldn't say.' Her voice was deadpan, disguising an uncharacteristic urge to scream. She'd been travelling for hours and right now she could do with a little of the famous regional hospitality and a minute or two to gather her wits. 'All I know is that his first concern was to ensure that you weren't left without assistance.'

His only response was an irritated grunt.

Okay, enough…

'Your cousin, His Highness the Emir of Ras al Kawi, will vouch for her bona fides,' she assured him, as if she was used to casually bandying about the names of the local royals. 'Her Highness Princess Violet entrusted Amanda with the task of finding her a nanny.'

'I don't need a nanny.'

'That's fortunate because I've never changed a nappy in my life.' Her reputation for calm under pressure was being put to the test and there had been an uncharacteristic snap to her response that earned her the fractional lift of an insolent brow.

'Miss Garland's note contains the names of some of the people I've worked for, should you require reassurance regarding my own capabilities,' she continued, calling on previously untested depths of calm.

'Will I have heard of them?' he asked, with heavy emphasis on *them*.

Since she had no way of knowing who he'd heard of, she assumed the question was not only sarcastic but rhetorical. Choosing not to risk another demonstration of the power of that eyebrow, she made no comment.

In the face of her silence he finally held out his hand for the letter, ripping open the flap with the broad tip of his thumb.

His face gave nothing away as he scanned the contents but he turned to the man holding her suitcase, spoke to him in Arabic before, with a last thoughtful look at her, he said, 'I'll see you in my office in fifteen minutes, Miss Dance.'

With that, he turned away, his leather flip-flops slapping irritably as he crossed the stone terrace before disappearing down steps that led to a lower level.

Shakily, Ruby let out her breath.

Whew. Double *whew*, with knobs on. Forget the grateful thanks for dropping everything and flying here at a moment's notice—that had been tense. On the other hand, now that he'd taken his naked torso out of sight and she could think clearly, she could understand his reluctance to take her at face value.

It wasn't personal.

Doubtless, there had been attempts to breach his security in the past, although whether for photographs of his isolated hideout, gossip on who he was sharing it with, or insider information on who was about to get the golden touch of Ansari financial backing was anyone's guess.

Any one of them would be worth serious money and an unexpected visitor was always going to get the hard stare and third degree. She, more than anyone, could understand that.

Easy to say—as she followed the servant through an ancient archway and down a short flight of steps, her skin was goosebumped, her breath catching in her throat—but it felt very personal.

At the bottom of the steps, sheltered from the sea by stone walls and from the heat of the summer by pergolas dripping with blue racemes of wisteria, scented with the tiny white stars of jasmine, was a terrace garden.

She stopped, entranced, her irritation melting away.

'*Madaam?*' the servant prompted, bringing her back to the reason she was there, and she turned to him.

'*Sho Ismak?*' She asked his name.

He smiled, bowed. '*Ismi* Khal, *madaam*.'

She placed her hand against her chest and said, '*Ismi*, Ruby.' Then, with a gesture at the garden, 'This is lovely. *Jameel*,' she said, calling on the little Arabic she'd learned during working trips to Dubai and Bahrain and topped up on the long flight from London.

'*Nam*. It is beautiful,' he said carefully, demonstrating his own English with a broad smile, before turning to open the door to a cool tiled lobby, slipping his feet from his sandals as he stepped inside.

She had no time to linger, admire the exquisite tiles decorating the walls, but, familiar with the customs of the region, she followed his example and slipped off her heels before padding after him.

He opened the door to a large, comfortably furnished sitting room, crossed the room to draw back shutters and open a pair of doors that led onto a small shaded area overlooking the sea. There was a rush of air, the scent of the sea mingled with jasmine and, despite the less than enthusiastic welcome and her own misgivings about coming here, she sighed with pleasure.

When Amanda had explained that Sheikh Ibrahim was sitting out his exile in a fort in Ras al Kawi, his maternal grandmother's native home, she had imagined something rugged, austere. It was all that, but below the ancient fortress a home, a garden, had been carved from the shelter of the hillside.

The man might be a grouch but this place was magical.

Khal was all set to give her the full guided tour of the suite, starting with the tiny kitchen, but she had just a few minutes to freshen up and get her head straight before she had to report to Sheikh Ibrahim.

'*Shukran*, Khal.' She tapped her watch to indicate that she was short of time. 'Where… *Ayn…?*' She mimed typing and he smiled, then took her to the door, pointed at the steps leading down.

'*Marra,*' he said, and held up one finger, then, '*Marrataan.*' Two fingers.

Once, twice?

'*Etnaan?* Two floors?'

He nodded, then rattled something off that she had no chance of understanding, before heading off down them.

Bram had showered on the beach when he came out of the sea but he stood in his wet room with cold water pouring off him while he caught his breath, recovered from that moment when he'd looked up and seen the dark, foreshortened silhouette of Ruby Dance against the sky and his heart had stopped.

In that split second he'd imagined every possible drama that would have brought Safia flying north to Ras al Kawi. To him. When Ruby Dance, and not Safia, had stepped out of the shadow, the complex rush of disappointment, guilt had hit him like a punch in the gut.

Her hair was the same dark silk as Safia's but it had been cut in short, feathery layers. Her eyes were not the rare blue-green that was the legacy of Iskandar's army, who'd fought and scattered their seed every inch of the way along the Gulf to India, but the cool blue-grey of a silver fox. She was a little taller and, while her voice had the same soft, low musical tones that wrapped around a man's heart, when she spoke it was with that clear precision—as English as a rainy day—of the privileged aristocratic women he'd known in Europe.

What she did have in common with Safia was a rare stillness, a face that gave no hint of what she was thinking or feeling.

Schooled to obedience—accepting without question a marriage arranged to keep the peace between their warring families when they were children—Safia would have played the role of perfect wife, borne his children, never by so much as a breath betraying her love for another man.

The arrival of a courier that morning bearing the summons home, and the difficult call from his brother, had stirred up long-buried memories, bringing Safia's image so vividly to mind that it had taken time for his brain to catch up with what his eyes were telling him. A seemingly endless moment when everything dead within him had stirred, quickened and he'd come close to taking her hand to draw her close. To step back five years and, if only for a moment, be the man he was meant to be. Husband, father, heir to his father's throne.

He shook his head, grabbed a towel and scrubbed at his face to erase the treacherous thought and concentrate on what Ruby Dance had said about Peter.

A badly broken leg, a wrist that would be out of action for weeks, the agony of cracked ribs; the timing couldn't be worse. There were a number of projects requiring his undivided attention and, after five long years of exile, the longed-for call home with a sting in the tail…

He glanced at the letter of introduction, picked up his phone and keyed Amanda Garland into the search engine.

Her reputation—clients who were prepared to publicly laud her to the skies, a Businesswoman of the Year award, an honour from Queen Elizabeth—

was as impressive as the list of people she'd offered as a reference.

He'd asked the Dance woman if he would have heard of any of them and the fact was that he'd met all of them. If she was used to working at this level she must be seriously good at her job and, unlike Peter, she wouldn't be itching to disappear into the desert for days at a time with a camera.

Ruby wasted no time in stripping off and stepping into the walk-in shower. She let the hard needles of water stream over her for one long minute, stimulating, refreshing, bringing her body back to life.

It was warmer here than in London, than on the air conditioned jet, and she abandoned her dark grey trouser suit in favour of a lightweight knee-length skirt and linen top. And, having already experienced the ancient steps, she slipped on a pair of black ballet flats.

She still had a few minutes and used them to check her phone for Amanda's text, copying the details of the hospital onto one of the index cards she carried with her before going in search of Sheikh Ibrahim's office.

The evening was closing in. The sea was flat calm, the sky ranging from deep purple in the east to pale pinks and mauves in the west while, in the shadows, tiny solar lights twined around the pergolas and set amongst the casual planting, were blinking on, shining through leaves, glinting on a ripple of water trickling down through rocks.

The garden had a quiet magic and she could have stood there for hours letting the peace seep into her bones. She took one last look then, out of time, she walked down to the next level where, in a corner, a few shrivelled fruits still clung to a pomegranate tree.

She found another flight of steps half hidden behind the thick stems of the bougainvillaea that softened the tower wall. These were narrower, skirting the cliff face with only a wall that did not reach the height of her shoulder to protect her from a nerve-tingling drop onto the rocks below. She did not linger and, precisely fifteen minutes later, as instructed by the Sheikh, she stepped down into a courtyard where concealed lights washed the walls, turning it into an outside room.

Sheikh Ibrahim, wet hair slicked back and now wearing shorts and a loose-fitting T-shirt that hung from those wide shoulders, was sitting, legs stretched out, ankles crossed on the footrest of an old-fashioned cane planters' chair, smartphone in hand.

There was a matching chair on the other side of the low table.

She placed the card with the hospital details in front of him, slid back the footrest on the empty chair, removed her phone, tablet, notepad and pen from her satchel and, tidily tucking her skirt beneath her, sat down.

He looked at her for what seemed like endless minutes, a slight frown buckling the space between his eyes.

Ruby had learned the habit of stillness long ago. It was her survival technique; she'd schooled herself not to blink, blanking even the most penetrating of stares with a bland look that had unnerved both the disapproving, pitying adults who didn't know what to say to her and the jeering classmates who knew only too well.

Perhaps she'd become complacent. It was a long time since anyone had bothered to look beyond the image of the professional peripatetic PA that she presented to the world. Now, sitting in front of Sheikh Ibrahim, waiting for him to say something, say anything, it took every ounce of concentration to maintain her composure.

Maybe it was the memory of water dripping onto his bare shoulder, running down his chest, the certainty that he'd been naked beneath that towel that was messing with her head.

Or that his thighs, calves, ankles honed to perfection on horseback, on the blackest of black ski runs, were everything hinted at beneath the jodhpurs he'd been wearing on the *Celebrity* cover she'd downloaded to the file she'd created as soon as Amanda had called her. Confirmed in the photograph of him cavorting naked in a London fountain, one arm around a girl in transparently wet underwear as he'd poured a bottle of champagne over them both. The photograph that had cost him a throne.

Or maybe it was that she recognised the darkness in his eyes, an all-consuming hunger for redemption. It crossed the space between them and a shiver rippled through her as if he'd reached out and touched her.

'Jude Radcliffe tells me that he offered you a permanent position in his organisation,' he said at last. 'Why didn't you take it?'

'You talked to Jude?' Amanda hadn't held back when it came to references.

'Is that a problem?' He spoke softly, inviting her confidence. She was not fooled. His voice might be seductively velvet but it cloaked steel.

'No, but it is Sunday. I didn't think he'd be at the office.'

'He wasn't. I know him well enough to call him at home.' His response was casual enough, but she didn't miss the underlying warning; someone he knew on a personal basis would be totally frank.

'Did he tell you that his wife was once a Garland temp?' she asked, demonstrating her own familiarity with the family. 'It's how they met. She was expecting her second baby the last time I worked at Radcliffe Tower.' She picked up her phone and checked her diary. 'It's due next month.'

'You keep files on the people you work for?'

She looked up. 'The way they like their coffee, their favoured airlines, the name of their hairdresser, shirt collar size, the brand of make-up they use, important birthdays. They're the small details that make me the person they call when their secretaries are sick,' she said. 'They're the reason why their PAs check whether I'll be available before they make their holiday bookings.'

'You don't undersell yourself. I'm surprised you were free to fly here at such short notice.'

'I'd taken a week's holiday to do some decorating.'

'Decorating?' he repeated, bemused.

'Paint, wallpaper?'

'You do it yourself?'

'Most people do.' Obviously not multimillionaire sheikhs.

'And at the end of the week?'

Was he suggesting a longer stay? The thought both excited and unsettled her. 'Shall we see how it goes?'

His eyes narrowed. 'Are you suggesting that I am on some kind of probationary period, Ruby Dance?'

Yes… At least, no…

For a moment there was no sound. A cicada

that had been tuning up intermittently fell silent, the waves lapping at the rocks below them stilled in that moment when the tide, suspended on the turn, paused to catch its breath.

She hadn't meant… Or maybe she had.

Deep breath, Ruby.

'My role is to provide emergency cover for as long as needed. A day, a week…I had assumed you would have someone to call on to stand in for Peter? Although…'

'Although?'

'If there had been anyone available to step into his shoes at a moment's notice I doubt he would have called his godmother.'

He gave her a thoughtful look but neither confirmed nor denied it, which suggested she was right.

'Do you have a file on me?' he asked.

Back on firmer ground, she flicked to the file she'd been compiling. 'It's missing a few details. I don't know your collar size,' she replied, looking up and inviting him to fill the gap in her records.

He shook his head. 'You are bluffing, Ruby Dance.'

'You like your coffee black with half a spoonful of Greek honey,' she replied. 'You have your own jet and helicopter—the livery is black with an A in Arabic script in gold on the tail—but, since you only travel once or twice a month, they are available for charter through Ansari Air, the company you set up for the purpose. The demand for this service apparently exceeded supply because you've since added two more executive jets and a second helicopter to your fleet. Should you need to travel when they are all busy you use Ramal Hamrah Airways, the airline owned by Sheikh Zahir al-Khatib, a cousin on your mother's side of the family. Your birthday is August the third, your father's birthday is…'

He held up a hand to stop her.

'The day after tomorrow.'

Amanda had passed on everything she knew about the man and the cabin crew on his private jet had been more than willing to share his likes and dislikes—anything, in fact, that would help her serve their boss. Like the entrepreneurs whose companies he had financed with start-up loans, they appeared to believe the sun shone out of the Sheikh's backside.

Perhaps he improved with acquaintance.

'You've made your point,' he admitted, 'but you haven't answered my question.'

'Jude offered me a very generous package as PA to his finance director,' she said, 'but I enjoy the variety offered by temping.'

Again there was that long, thoughtful look and for a moment she was sure he was going to challenge her on a response so ingrained, repeated so often, that she had almost come to believe it. His perceptiveness did not surprise her. A man who'd made a fortune in a few short years as a venture capitalist would need to read more than a business plan; he would have to be fluent in body language.

Under the circumstances, a man looking for a hidden agenda might well read her give-nothing-away stillness as a red flag and, since he wasn't about to divulge his collar size, she leaned forward and put the phone down.

'Radcliffe urged me to make other arrangements before the end of May,' Sheikh Ibrahim continued after a moment. 'He mentioned a wedding.' His glance dropped to her hand.

'Not mine.'

'No, I can see that you already wear a wedding ring. Your husband does not object to you working away from home?'

Her fingers tightened protectively against the plain gold band she wore on her right hand, the hand on which she knew they wore wedding rings—if they wore them at all—in this part of the world.

'It's a family ring,' she said. 'My grandmother wore it. And my mother. If I were married I would wear it on my left hand.' She looked up but he said nothing and she knew that he could not have cared less whether or not she was married or what her husband thought about her absences. That was the reason she temped. She was here today, gone tomorrow and no one, not even the person she was working for, had the time or inclination to concern themselves with her personal life. 'I'm booked to cover Jude's PA,' she said. 'She's getting married at the beginning of June. Hopefully, Peter Hammond's leg will be up to all these steps by then.'

Sheikh Ibrahim was saved from answering by the appearance of Khal, carrying a tray, which he placed in front of her.

'*Shaay, madaam*,' he said, indicating a small silver teapot.

'*Shukran*, Khal.' She indicated a second pot. 'And this?'

'That is mint tea,' Sheikh Ibrahim said before he could answer. 'I'm surprised you don't have a note of my preference in your file.'

'My files are always a work in progress, but I do have a note that, unusually, you take it without sugar. Would you like some now, Sheikh?'

'We're on first name terms here.' If her knowledge irritated him he kept the fact well hidden. 'Everyone calls me Bram.'

She was on first name terms with most of the men and women she temped for on a regular basis, but she hadn't seen any of them half naked.

It shouldn't matter, but somehow it did.

She glanced up at the sky, the stars beginning to blink on as the hood of darkness moved swiftly over them from the east, and took a steadying breath. When she looked back it occurred to her that she wasn't the only one struggling to hold onto at least the appearance of relaxation. She was pretty fluent in body language herself and, despite the way he was stretched out in that chair, he was, like her, coiled as tight as a spring.

'Would you like tea, Bram?' she managed, hoping that the slight wobble was just in her head.

Their gazes met and for a moment she felt dizzy. It wasn't his powerful thighs, shapely calves, those long sinewy feet stretched out in front of her like temptation. It was his eyes, although surely that dark glowing amber had to be a trick of the light? Or maybe she was hallucinating in the scent-laden air?

CHAPTER TWO

A PING FROM her phone warning her of an incoming text broke the tension. Bram nodded and, miraculously, Ruby managed to pour mint tea into a tall glass set in a silver holder and place it in front of him without incident.

As if he too needed a distraction, he reached for the card on which she'd written the hospital details, murmured something.

'I'm sorry?'

He shook his head. 'He's in Gstaad. I broke my ankle there years ago.'

'Remind me never to go there. It's clearly a dangerous place,' she added when he gave her a blank look.

Her Internet search for information had thrown up dozens of photographs of him in skin-hugging Lycra, hurtling down vertiginous ski runs, and with the resulting medals around his neck.

'Maybe,' he said, his eyes distant, no doubt thinking of a different life when he'd been a champion, a media darling, a future king.

'I'm sorry.'

He didn't ask her what she was sorry for and in truth she didn't know. If he wanted to ski, play polo, there was nothing to stop him, other than shame for having disgraced his family. Was giving it all up, leaving his A-list social life in Europe to live in this isolated place, atonement for scandalising the country he had been born to serve?

Or did he want the throne of Umm al Basr more than the rush of competition, the prizes and the glamorous women who hung around the kind of men who attracted photographers?

Was the hunger at the back of his eyes the need for forgiveness or determination to regain all he had lost?

He dropped the card back on the table.

'Call the hospital. Make sure they have all the details of Peter's medical insurance and tell them that whatever he needs above and beyond that he is to have. Talk to his mother,' he continued as she made a note on her pad. 'Liaise with her about flying him back to England as soon as he's able to travel. Make sure that there is a plane at their disposal and arrange for a private ambulance to pick him up and take him wherever he needs to go.'

She made another note. 'Is there any message?'

'You're a clumsy oaf?' he suggested, but without the smile that should have accompanied his suggestion.

She looked up. 'Will there be flowers with that?'

'What do you think?'

What she thought was that Peter Hammond

hadn't crashed his snowboard for the sole purpose of annoying his boss although, if she'd been him, she might have been tempted to take a dive into the snow rather than spend one more day working for Bram Ansari.

What she said was, 'Get well soon is more traditional under the circumstances, but it's undoubtedly a man thing. I'm sure he'll get the message.'

She certainly did but, despite the cool reception, she had some sympathy. It was bad enough to have your routine disrupted by the drama of outside events without having a total stranger thrust into your life and, in Bram Ansari's case, his home.

He might be an arrogant jerk but she was there to ensure that Peter's absence did not disturb his life more than absolutely necessary and she was professional enough to make that happen, with or without his co-operation. Not that she'd waste her breath saying so. The first few hours were show-not-tell time.

'No doubt he'll be as anxious to be back on his feet as you are for his return,' she said as she picked up the card and tucked it into her notebook. 'Unfortunately, bones can't be hurried.'

'I'm aware of that but Peter manages the day-to-day running of Qa'lat al Mina'a. Without him we don't eat.'

'Everything is flown in from the city, I imagine.' She could handle that. It wouldn't be the first time that running a house had come within the remit of an assignment. 'What did people do here before?'

'Before?'

'Before there was a city with an air-conditioned mall selling luxuries flown in from around the world. Before there were helicopters to deliver your heart's desire to places such as this.'

He shrugged. 'They fished, kept livestock and there were camels to bring rice, spices, everything else.' He gave her another of those thoughtful looks. 'Have you ever wrung a chicken's neck, Ruby? Or slaughtered a goat?'

'Why?' she asked, not about to make his day with girlish squealing. 'Is that included in the job description?'

'There is no job description. Peter has an open-ended brief encompassing whatever is necessary.'

He was challenging her, she realised. Demanding to know if she was up to the job.

Clearly the quiet diligence she usually found most helpful when dealing with a difficult employer wasn't going to work here, but they were stuck with each other until one of them cracked and summoned the helicopter.

'You're saying you make it up as you go along?' she asked, lobbing it right back because it wasn't ever going to be her. She couldn't afford the luxury.

'Is there a better way?'

'Personally, I'm working to a five-year plan,' she said, 'but, for the record, exactly how many goats has Peter Hammond slaughtered?'

A glint appeared in those amber eyes and a crease deepened at the corner of Bram Ansari's mouth. Not a smile, nothing like a smile; more a warning that she was living dangerously. Not that she needed it. She'd been aware of the danger from the moment she'd first set eyes on him.

'One?' she suggested. Then, when he didn't answer, 'Two?' Still nothing. 'More than two?'

'So far,' he admitted, 'he's managed to dodge that bullet by ensuring that the freezer is always fully stocked.'

'Much less messy,' she agreed briskly, 'and I'm sure the goats are grateful for his efficiency. If you'll point me in the direction of his office I'll attempt to follow his example.' Apparently she'd won that round because his only response was to wave a hand in the direction of a pair of open glazed doors leading from the terrace. 'And your office?'

'My office is wherever I happen to be.'

Having dished out the if-you're-so-damned-good-get-on-with-it treatment, he leaned back in the chair and closed his eyes.

She wasn't entirely convinced by his relaxed dismissal—she had won that round on points—but she picked up her glass, crossed the terrace, flipped on the light and kicked off her shoes as she entered Peter Hammond's office. She half expected to find a man cave but it was uncluttered, austere in its simplicity.

A huge rug, jewel-coloured and silky beneath her feet, covered the flagstone floor. The walls were bare ancient stone, hung with huge blow-ups of stunning black and white photographs: weathered rock formations; the spray of a waterfall frozen in a moment in time and so real that if she put a hand out she might feel it splashing through her fingers; a close-up of the suspicious eye of a desert oryx.

The only furniture was a battle-scarred desk and a good chair. The only item on the desk was a slender state-of-the-art laptop which, no doubt, had the protection of an equally state-of-the-art password.

She put her cup and bag on the desk, opened up the laptop and, sure enough, she got the prompt.

It wasn't the first time she'd been faced with this situation and she reached for the pull-out ledge under the desk top—the classic place to jot down passwords.

Nothing. While she approved of Peter Hammond's security savvy, on this occasion she would have welcomed a little carelessness. No doubt Bram Ansari was, at that moment, lying back in his recliner amusing himself by counting down the seconds until she called for help.

She sat down, checked the drawers.

They were not locked, but contained nothing more revealing than the fact that he had a weakness for liquorice allsorts and excellent taste in pens and notebooks.

A walk-in cupboard at the rear of the office contained shelves holding a supply of stationery on one wall and a neat array of box files. Against the other wall was a table containing a printer and a scanner.

She took down the file labelled 'Medical Insurance', carried it to the desk and, having found the relevant paperwork, discovered that there wasn't a phone. Of course not. There was no landline here—Bram had been holding the latest in smartphones, the same model as her own—and Peter would have his mobile phone with him.

Not a problem. She took her own phone from her bag—the cost of her calls would be added to his account—and saw the waiting text. Number unknown.

She clicked on it and read.

Amanda gave me your number, Ruby, so that I could give you the password for Peter's laptop.

It's pOntefr@c! Can you let me have the details of his medical insurance when you have a moment? Good luck! Elizabeth Hammond.

She grinned. Pontefract—where the liquorice came from.

She tried it and was in.

'Bless the man!' she said and called Elizabeth Hammond to pass on the insurance details, along with the rest of Bram Ansari's instructions.

'Heaven's, that was quick, Ruby. You're clearly as hot as Amanda said.'

If only the rest of the 'open-ended brief' was as simple…

'If there's any other information you need just call me on this number,' she said. 'How is Peter?'

'Sore but the breaks were clean and should heal without any permanent damage.'

'That is good news. Sheikh Ibrahim said to tell him that he's a clumsy oaf, which I assume is man-speak for get well soon.'

'It's going to be weeks, I'm afraid.'

'Weeks?'

'Can you manage that? Bram Ansari is…' She paused, called out to someone that she was coming, then said, 'I'm sorry, Ruby, but I ordered room service and it has just arrived. Thanks again for all your help.'

Ruby, phone at her cheek, wondered what Elizabeth Hammond had been about to say when she'd been interrupted.

Bram Ansari is difficult to work for? Bram Ansari is a pain in the butt? Bram Ansari is very easy on the eye?—a fact which did not cancel out the first two. She knew, no one better, that attractiveness, charm, in a man could hide a multitude of sins.

Obviously, she had no concerns on the charm front.

Bram watched from beneath hooded lids as Ruby Dance picked up her glass and disappeared into Peter's office.

Something about her bothered him and it wasn't just that first shocking moment when he'd thought she was Safia. It was nothing that he could put his finger on. She was clearly good at her job if a little waspish. No doubt she was simply responding to his own mood; Jude Radcliffe, not a man to bestow praise lightly, had said that he was very lucky that she'd been free. Apparently she had a memory like an elephant, was cool-headed in a crisis and was as tight-lipped as a clam. She certainly hadn't been fazed by his clumsy attempt to unsettle her, to get a feeling for the woman hiding behind that cool mask.

On the contrary, he felt as if he'd been in a

fencing match and was lucky to have got away with a draw.

Only once he'd caught a momentary flash of irritation in those cool grey eyes. Such control was rare, a learned skill. That she'd taken the trouble to master it suggested that she had something to hide.

He thumbed her name into a search engine but all he came up with was a dance studio. That, too, was unusual. His curiosity aroused, he called up the security program he used when he ran an initial check on someone who was looking for financial backing. Again nothing.

No social media presence, no borrowing, not even a credit rating, which implied that she didn't have a credit card. Or maybe not one in that name. It was definitely time to go and check what she was up to in Peter's office.

He'd just swung his feet to the floor when his phone rang.

'Bram?'

The voice was sleepy, a bit slurred, but unmistakable.

'Peter…' No point in asking how he was; he would be floating on the residue of anaesthesia. 'I suppose you were trying to impress some leggy chalet maid?'

'You've got me,' he said, a soft chuckle abruptly shortened into an expletive as his ribs gave him a sharp reminder that it was no laughing matter. 'Next time I'll stay in bed and let her impress me.'

'Good decision. What's the prognosis?'

'Boredom, physio, boredom, physio. Repeat until done… What's the Garland Girl like?'

'Garland Girl?'

'That's what they were called before it became politically incorrect to call anyone over the age of ten a girl. She did turn up, didn't she? I told Amanda that it was urgent. Tried to tell you but your phone was busy and then…' He hesitated, clearly trying to remember what had happened next.

'Don't worry about it. She's here and right now staring at your laptop wondering where you hid your password. I was on my way to rescue her when you rang.'

'She won't need you to rescue her,' he said. 'Garland temps are the keyboard queens, the crème de la crème of the business world. Her job is to rescue you. Ask m'father,' he said. 'M'mother was one…' He coughed, swore again. 'She sends her love, by the way.'

'Please give her my best wishes. Is your father there?' he asked.

'He's at the UN until next week. Why?' he said, suddenly sharper. 'Is there a problem?' When he was too slow to deny it Peter said, 'What's happened?'

'Well, the good news is that I have received an invitation to my father's birthday *majlis*.'

'And the bad news is that Ahmed Khadri will gut you the moment he sets eyes on you.'

'Apparently not. Hamad phoned to warn me that my father has done a secret deal with Khadri. Safia hasn't given my brother a son and they're impatient for an heir with Khadri blood. The price of my return is marriage to Bibi Khadri, Safia's youngest sister.'

Peter's soft expletive said it all. 'There's more than one way to gut a man…'

'He wins, whichever way I jump. If I go, he has more influence in court as well as the eye-watering dowry he will demand from me. If I stay away, my father will take it as a personal insult and any chance of a reconciliation will be lost. I doubt Khadri can make up his mind which outcome would please him most.'

'Who knows about this?'

'No one. Hamad only found out because Bibi managed to smuggle a note to her sister.'

He was not the only one to be horrified by such a match.

'Okay… So if you turned up with a wife in tow—'

'You're rambling, Peter. Go to sleep.'

'Not a real wife. A temp,' he said. 'And, by

happy coincidence, you happen to have one handy… Ask the Garland Girl.'

Ruby put the phone down, turned to the laptop and began to go through Peter's diary, printing off each entry for the following week. She had collected the sheets from the printer, sorted them and clipped them into a folder when a shadow across the door warned her that she was no longer alone.

'I realised that you didn't have the password to Peter's laptop but I see that you've found it. Did he have it written down somewhere obvious?' he asked.

She counted to three before she looked up. Bram Ansari was leaning against the doorjamb, arms folded, but there was an intense watchfulness in his eyes that belied the casual stance.

'No,' she said.

'No, not obvious?'

'No, he didn't have it written down.'

'And yet you are in. Should I be worried?'

Ruby was seriously tempted to leave it at that and let him wonder how she'd done it. She resisted. He'd taken his time about it but he had eventually turned up and playing mind games was not the way to build a working relationship. She took pride in the fact that when she had worked for someone she always got a call back.

'I'm good, Bram, but I'm not that good. Peter asked his mother to text it to me.'

'I was just talking to him. He didn't mention it.'

'Maybe he forgot. Or maybe he wanted to make me look amazingly efficient. How is he?'

'High on the lingering remains of anaesthetic. Talking too much when he should be resting.'

'Did you rest?' she asked. 'When you broke your ankle?'

His shoulders moved in the merest suggestion of a shrug. 'Boredom is the mother of invention.'

His smile was little more than a tug on the corner of his mouth, deepening the droop, but it felt as if he had included her in a private joke and her own lips responded all by themselves. And not just her lips. Little pings of recognition lit up in parts of her body that had lain dormant, unused, not wanted in this life. Definitely not wanted here.

'He rang to make sure that you'd arrived safely and to tell me how lucky I am to have you.'

'What a nice man,' she said. 'I'll send him a box of liquorice allsorts.'

'It didn't take you long to discover his weakness.'

'One I confess that I share.' He didn't respond and, feeling rather foolish, she said, 'I've spoken to Mrs Hammond and passed on all the information she needed.' He nodded. 'It's going to be weeks before Peter will be able to manage all these steps.'

'He won't be coming back.' She frowned. 'His father was Ambassador to Umm al Basr when Peter was a boy. He loves the desert and when he dropped out of university, didn't know what to do with himself, I asked him if he wanted to come here and give me a hand. I'd given financial backing to a friend who wanted to go into commercial production with winter sports equipment—'

'Maxim de Groote.'

'Is that in your file too?' he asked.

'It's all over the Internet.'

'I don't use social media.' He shook his head, as if the interest of other people in his life bewildered him.

She wasn't convinced. This was a man whose naked romp in a fountain, caught on someone's phone, had gone viral on social media networks before the police arrived to arrest him.

'When he publicly floated his company Maxim told a journalist that he owed everything to you,' she said. 'Did he?'

'No, he owed it to his own vision and hard work.'

'And the fact that you had the faith to invest in him.'

'I knew him,' he said, 'but I was immediately inundated with would-be entrepreneurs looking for capital. Peter was going to stay for a few weeks and do the thanks-but-no-thanks replies while he thought about his future.'

'But that didn't happen.'

'He would insist on reading the crazier ideas out loud and one of them caught my interest. The rest, as they say, is history.' He shrugged as if his ability to pick winners was nothing. 'Peter stayed because it suited him at the time.' He gestured towards the photographs. 'These days he spends more time out in the desert with his camera than at his desk.'

'Peter is the photographer? He's very talented.'

'And it's time he got serious about it. If I hadn't been so busy I would have kicked him out a year ago. The fact that he had Amanda Garland's number to hand suggests that he'd been working on an exit strategy of his own.' He nodded at the folder she was holding. 'What have you got there?'

She glanced at it. 'It's your detailed diary for tomorrow and a summary for the week. I wasn't sure how Peter handled it. I usually print out a list.'

'Run me through it,' he said, finally leaving the doorway and crossing to her desk.

'You have a conference call booked with Roger Pei in Hong Kong tomorrow morning and there's a reminder that you should call Susan Graham in New York before Wall Street opens.' She went through a list of other calls he was both expecting and planned to make. 'The times and numbers are all there.'

'And the rest of the week?'

'You have video conferences booked every day this week, you're flying to Dubai on Wednesday and there's a charity dinner here in Ras al Kawi hosted by His Highness Sheikh Fayad and Princess Violet tomorrow evening.'

'I can't miss that,' he said, taking the folder from her and checking the entry. 'Have you got anything to wear?'

'Wear?'

'Something suitable for a formal dinner.'

She felt her carefully controlled air of calm—which hadn't buckled under the suggestion that she might have to slaughter a goat—slip a notch. But then she hadn't taken that threat seriously.

'You want me to go with you?' Meetings, conferences, receptions were all grist to her mill, but she'd never been asked to accompany any of the men she'd worked for to a black tie dinner. They had partners for that. Partners with designer wardrobes, accessories costing four figures, jewellery…

Perhaps sensing her reluctance, he looked up from the diary page. 'It comes under the "whatever is necessary" brief. You were serious about that, Ruby?' he asked, regarding her with a quiet intensity that sent a ripple of apprehension coursing through her veins.

'Whatever is necessary within the parameters of legal, honest and decent,' she said, hoping that the smile made it through to her face.

He handed back the diary. 'Call Princess Violet's office and ask her assistant to send you some dresses from her latest collection.'

'I have a dress,' she said quickly. Even the simplest of Princess Violet al Kuwani's designer gowns would cost more than she earned in a month.

'Let me guess,' he said. 'It's black.'

Black was practical and her capsule wardrobe had been created to cover all eventualities, although she hadn't anticipated wearing anything so formal on this assignment.

'A simple black dress will take you anywhere,' she told him. 'It's the female equivalent of a dinner jacket.'

'So it's a boring black dress.'

'I'll be working, not flirting.'

'I'm glad you understand that.' He held her gaze for a moment then said, 'There has been a development that will involve rescheduling some of those appointments, but first we will eat.'

No, no, no...

No socialising in the workplace. No getting into situations where people would ask where she came from, about her family, all the conversational gambits used to probe who you were and where you would fit into the social layers of their lives.

She didn't do 'social'.

'Come,' he said, extending a hand towards her, and for the first time since she'd arrived she saw not the A-list pin-up, the sportsman, the venture capitalist, but a man born to command, a prince. 'Bring the diary with you.'

The diary. Right. It was a working dinner. Of course it was. He only wanted her with him to keep track of who he spoke to, the appointments he made. That she could handle and, fortifying herself with a steadying breath, she gathered her things and headed for the door and that outstretched hand.

She was sure he was going to place it at her back, maybe take her arm as they descended the worn, uneven steps. He waited until she passed him, closed the door behind them and, having held herself rigid, knowing that no matter how much she tried to relax she would still jump at his touch, she felt a weird jolt of disappointment when he simply paused beside her.

Disappointment was bad.

She looked up, anywhere but at him.

During the short time she had been working, every trace of light had left the sky. Above them stars were glittering diamond-bright in a clear black sky, but she was too strung up to look for the constellations; all her senses were focused on the man beside her. The warmth of his body so close to hers. The scent of the sea air clinging to his skin overlaid with the tiny flowers that had fallen on his shoulders as he brushed past a jasmine vine.

No...

The word clanged in her brain so loudly that when Bram glanced at her she thought he must have heard.

It wasn't as if she even liked the man but it was pointless to pretend that she was immune to the magnetic quality that had once made him a *Celebrity* cover favourite.

Work, she reminded herself. She was here to work.

Concentrate on the job.

'What's your routine?' she asked in her briskly efficient PA voice as he led the way down to a lower level, determined to blot out emergency signals from synapses that hadn't been this excited in years.

'Routine?' He frowned, as if it was a word alien to his vocabulary.

'What time are you normally at your desk? I imagine it's earlier than London.'

'Peter usually goes for a run or swim at first

light, has breakfast and if he's not chasing the light with his camera he deals with overnight emails.' He glanced down at her. 'Do you run, Ruby?'

'Only for a bus.' She'd hoped to raise a smile, lessen the tension, but there was no noticeable reaction.

'Swim?'

She glanced across the tumble of walls, courtyards, to the dark water sucking at the foot of the fort. 'Not in the sea.'

'There is a pool.' If he'd noticed her involuntary shiver, he made no comment. 'There's also a fully equipped gym if you prefer.'

'No, thanks.' She'd already seen him wet from the sea and she wasn't about to risk walking in on him slicked with sweat. 'I keep in shape by walking to work when I can, using the stairs instead of the lift and taking a weekly tap dancing class.' He gave her another of those looks. Assessing, unnerving… 'It's cheaper than a gym membership and the shoes are prettier,' she said quickly.

'There's no shortage of steps here.' His smile, unexpected as the sun on a winter morning—he knew how to smile?—took her by surprise. For a moment her foot hung in mid-air and then, as she missed the step, she flung out her hands, grabbing for something—anything—to hang onto and found herself face first in Bram Ansari's washed soft T-shirt, nestled against the hard-muscled shoulder it concealed. Drowning in the scent of sun-dried laundry and warm skin as he caught her, held her.

'Sorry,' she mumbled in a rush of embarrassed heat, jerking back from the intimacy of the contact. 'Apparently I can't walk and talk at the same time.'

'The steps are old, uneven.' Her head might have made a bid to escape the mortifying closeness but the rest of her was pressed against hard thighs, a washboard-flat stomach, her breasts pinioned against the broad chest that she was picturing all too vividly. 'Maybe you should stick to swimming while you're here,' he said, moving his hands to her shoulders and, still holding her steady, taking a step back. 'If you didn't bring a costume then send for one. You'll be glad of it when the weather heats up.'

Forget the weather. Bram Ansari was creating all the heat she could handle.

'It seems hardly worth it for a week.'

They had reached a point where the steps narrowed and he'd taken the lead so that when he stopped, turned, he was looking directly into her eyes.

'And if I need more than a week?'

Ruby had been a temp for a long time and she knew that there were people you had to flatter, those you had to mother and those rare and wonderful individuals who just got on with it and required nothing from you except your ability to keep things running smoothly in a crisis. Then there were the ones you had face down, never showing the slightest hint of weakness, never showing by as much as the flicker of an eyelash what you were feeling.

It had been clear from the moment that she'd set eyes on him that Sheikh Ibrahim al-Ansari fitted the latter description. Ignoring the battalion of butterflies battering against her breastbone, she looked right back at him and said, 'At this rate I'll be surprised if I'm here for more than twenty-four hours.'

They continued to stare at one another for the longest ten seconds in her life and then he said, 'Is that it or have you run out of smart answers?'

'I wouldn't count on it.'

This time his smile was no more than a tiny contraction of the lines fanning out from eyes that said nothing but it softened his face and had much the same effect on her knees.

'No...' For a moment he seemed lost for words. 'Shall we eat?'

'Good idea. With my mouth full I'll be less likely to put my foot in it.'

His smile deepened and it was probably a good thing that he placed his hand beneath her elbow, keeping her safe as they continued down the steps. *Probably.* She wouldn't fall, but her skin shimmered with the intimacy of his touch and she didn't let out her breath until they stepped down onto a terrace from which wide steps led down to the beach and he finally let go.

A table had been laid with a white cloth, flowers, candles sheltered within glass globes, sleek modern silver cutlery. The only sound was the lulling ripple of the sea, the shushing of the sand moving as the tide began to recede.

The scene was seductively exotic, a long way from the usual end to her working day. Khal gave her a wide smile as he held out a chair for her then, when she was settled, he turned to Bram and asked him a question.

For a moment the conversation went back and forth until finally Bram said, 'Antares.'

'Ruby?' Khal asked, turning to her and evidently expecting her to understand what he'd said.

'Khal is asking if you wish to ride in the morning.'

'Ride?'

The soft, fizzing intimacy of the moment shattered and in an instant she was in the past, hugging the fat little Shetland pony that had arrived on her fourth birthday, the feel of his thick, shaggy mane beneath her fingers, the smell of new leather.

'Do you ride?' Bram prompted when she took too long to answer.

Ruby forced a smile. 'Not for years and, in view of what happened to Peter, I promised Amanda that I wouldn't take part in any dangerous sports while I was here.'

'Life is a dangerous sport, Ruby.' He held her gaze for a moment, a questioning kink to his brow, but when she said nothing he turned back to Khal, said a few words in Arabic.

The man bowed, wished them both goodnight and left them to their supper.

'Antares?' she asked as she picked up her napkin and laid it on her lap, determined to keep the conversation impersonal. 'You name your horses after the stars?'

'Only the brightest ones. Antares, Rigel, Vega, Hadar, Altair, Adhara. They were my polo string.' He shook his head. 'I should have sold them when I left England. They're getting fat and lazy.'

'It's hard. They become an extension of you,' she said. 'Part of the family.' Her mother had wanted to sell her ponies as she grew out of them but she'd pleaded with her father and they had all stayed, eating their heads off and costing a fortune in vet's bills.

His look was thoughtful—so much for keeping it impersonal—but a woman appeared with a tray and he said, 'Ruby, this is Mina. She is an extraordinary cook but she only has a few words of English. Her husband, son and daughter-in-law take care of the fort for me.'

'*As-salaam alaykum*, Mina.'

Mina responded with a rush of Arabic and a broad smile. 'She's very happy to meet you,' Bram said, filling their glasses from a jug of juice. 'You have some Arabic?'

'I've worked in Bahrain and Dubai so I picked up a few words. Amanda assured me that you worked in English but I assumed all the staff would be Arabic speaking so I downloaded a basic course to my tablet. It was a long flight.'

'The legend is true then.'

'Legend?'

'Peter suggested that to have a Garland Girl as a personal assistant or nanny is considered something of a status symbol.'

She rolled her eyes. 'A newspaper did a profile on Amanda's agency years ago and came up with that ghastly name. They made us sound like the office equivalent of the Playboy Bunny.'

His jaw tightened as he fought a grin.

'It's okay,' she said, 'you can laugh. I'm twenty-seven. No one's idea of a girl,' she said. 'Or a bunny.'

'There is no right answer to that,' he said, offering her a plate. 'Have one of these.'

She took one of the hot, crispy little pastries

without comment. It was filled with goat's cheese and as she bit into it Ruby almost groaned with pleasure. They had to be about a million calories each, but she told herself that she'd work them off walking up and down all those steps.

'You approve?'

'They are scrumptious.'

'That's a word I haven't heard in a while. If I had to make a guess, I'd say you went to one of those exclusive boarding schools where the British upper classes park their children.'

The kind of women whose social calendar would include afternoons at Smith's Lawn watching as princes whacked a ball with a polo stick, and après-ski parties in Gstaad…

'What is this? Tit for tat?' she asked, with a smile to disguise the fact that she'd changed the subject. 'I know how you like your coffee so you checked me out online?'

'And if I had, Ruby Dance,' he replied, his voice softer than a Dartmoor mist and twice as dangerous, that almost-smile a trap for the unwary, 'what would I have found?'

Her skin prickled, her mouth dried.

He had…

Despite Jude's reference, despite the fact that Peter Hammond was Amanda's godson, he'd put her name into a search engine and knew exactly what he would find.

'Not very much,' she admitted.

'Not very much suggests that there would be something,' he pointed out, 'but there was no social media, no credit history and no Ruby Dance who was born twenty-seven years ago.' He sat back in his chair. 'I could dig deeper and unearth your secrets, but why don't you save me the bother and tell me who you really are?'

Protected by the reputation of the Garland Agency, her anonymity as a temp, this was the first time anyone had ever bothered to question Ruby's bona fides and the air rang with the silence as she tried to marshal her thoughts.

She wasn't fooled by the casual way he'd asked the question.

She'd been joking when she'd suggested that she'd last no more than twenty-four hours. Apparently the joke was on her because she wasn't going to be able to brush this aside, laugh it off as an aversion to the rush to tell everyone what she had for breakfast, of sharing pictures of cute kittens, as an excuse for her low profile.

He'd already gone far deeper than social media, was certain that she had not been born Ruby Dance, and the less he found the more suspicious he would become.

She unstuck her tongue from the roof of her mouth and said, 'I changed my name for family reasons.'

'A clause in a will? Your mother remarried?' he suggested.

She shook her head. He was dangling easy answers before her. Testing her. 'There was a scandal involving my father. Newspaper headlines. Reporters digging around in dustbins and paying the neighbours for gossip.'

He raised an eyebrow, inviting her to continue.

'Amanda Garland knows my history,' she said, 'and her reputation stands on trust.'

'Trust her, trust you—is that the deal?'

Her throat was dry and the juice gleamed enticingly but she resisted the urge to grab for it, swallow a mouthful. 'That's the deal.'

'And that's why you continue to temp rather than accept a permanent job? For the anonymity?'

'Yes…' The word stuck like a lump of wood in her throat.

'Where is your father now, Ruby?'

'He's dead. He and my mother died when I was seventeen.'

'Do you have any other family?'

'No.' She shook her head. 'I was the only child of only children.' At least as far as she knew. Her father might have had a dozen children…

'Can I ask if you are in any kind of relationship?' he persisted.

'Relationship?'

'You are on your own—you have no ties?'

He was beginning to spook her and must have realised it because he said, 'I have a proposition for you, Ruby, but if you have personal commitments…' He shook his head as if he wasn't sure what he was doing.

'If you're going to offer me a package too good to refuse after a couple of hours I should warn you that it took Jude Radcliffe the best part of a year to get to that point and I still turned him down.'

'I don't have the luxury of time,' he said, 'and the position I'm offering is made for a temp.'

'I'm listening.'

'Since you have done your research, you know that I was disinherited five years ago.'

She nodded. She thought it rather harsh for a one-off incident but the media loved the fall of a hero and had gone into a bit of a feeding frenzy.

'This morning I received a summons from my father to present myself at his birthday *majlis*.'

'You can go home?'

'If only it were that simple. A situation exists which means that I can only return to Umm al Basr if I'm accompanied by a wife.'

She ignored the slight sinking feeling in her stomach. Obviously a multimillionaire who looked like the statue of a Greek god—albeit one who'd suffered a bit of wear and tear—would have someone ready and willing to step up to the plate.

'That's rather short notice. Obviously, I'll do

whatever I can to arrange things, but I don't know a lot about the law in—'

'The marriage can take place tomorrow. My question is, under the terms of your open-ended brief encompassing "whatever is necessary", are you prepared to take on the role?'

CHAPTER THREE

'ME?'

Bram let go of the breath he'd been holding as Ruby reached for the glass of juice. Her hand was shaking but, rather than throwing it at him, she lifted it to her lips. She was taking a moment to gather her thoughts and he did not interrupt them.

'You're suggesting that I pretend to be your wife.'

'No.' He was a fairly shrewd judge of character and everything she'd done and said suggested she would appreciate straight talking, but there was no way of knowing how she'd take such an outrageous suggestion. 'What I'm suggesting is a temporary marriage of convenience with the divorce, at a mutually convenient moment, as easily arranged as the wedding.'

The dark arch of Ruby's brow hit her hairline. 'But you don't know me...'

'I don't have to know you. That's the deal with a temp and, as you've been at pains to stress, you are a temp with the highest references.'

'As a temporary PA!'

'I still need one of those.'

'But the marriage would be real?'

'There will have to be a contract witnessed by

someone my father trusts but, to be quite clear, this will be a simple business arrangement with a title upgrade from temporary personal assistant to temporary princess. While the pay grade is on a scale to match the new position, there would be no additional duties.'

'By *additional duties* you mean sex?' she said. 'To be absolutely clear.'

She was direct; he'd give her that. 'No sex,' he assured her. If this was to work it had to be a business arrangement. No complications.

'You simply want to convince your father that you're married.' She sat back in her chair, sitting holding the juice 'Are you gay, Bram?'

Direct? That was direct…

'I realise that in some parts of the world it's difficult,' she continued. Her face might be made for poker but he could imagine the thoughts racing through her brain. The real nature of his relationship with Peter…

'No!' He stopped as Mina appeared. She spoke little English but she understood the word no, and thought he was telling her to wait, but he quickly reassured her and when she had removed their empty plates he said, 'No, Ruby, I'm not gay but if I was I wouldn't hide the fact behind a paper marriage.'

'So what are you hiding?'

'There are pressing reasons, Ruby.'

'No doubt.' Those wide silver eyes were fixed on him and the drop in temperature of her voice was like a cold draught. 'I'm sorry, Sheikh, but I can't be party to such a deception.' A draught cold enough to be coming off the Russian Steppes in January.

The fact that she'd turned him down flat was no more than he had expected and only served to prove everything that Jude and Peter had told him about her.

'My father had heart bypass surgery last year, Ruby.'

Her eyes softened. 'I didn't know. I'm sorry—'

'He refuses to step down, rest. I have to be there to kneel at his feet, receive his forgiveness.'

'And he will want you there.' She paused as Mina returned with plates, more food, urging them to eat. 'I don't understand what the problem is,' she said, as she spooned spiced chicken and rice onto his plate and then hers. 'He's the Emir. His word is law.'

'A ruler has to put aside personal feelings for the good of his people. Umm al Basr was once torn apart by tribal infighting and no one cared until oil was found. The prospect of wealth focused everyone's minds and a meeting of the tribal elders chose the Ansari family as their leader. The Khadri family were soothed with a marriage contract, a political alliance between the oldest daughter of the Khadri family and the future Emir of Umm al Basr, joining the bloodline in a pact to end decades of discord.'

'The medieval solution. Seal a peace deal with the sacrifice of a daughter.'

'I was ten years old and Safia Khadri was four at the time the contract was written. When I dishonoured Safia with my escapade in the fountain, Ahmed Khadri threatened to kill me if I ever set foot in Umm al Basr.'

'A bit excessive?' She was toying with her food now. 'Presumably he was seizing a handy excuse to cause trouble and stir up feelings against your family?'

He smiled. 'You are very quick, Ruby. I do not place my life at so great a value, but my death would have had to be avenged and that would have meant a return to the kind of tribal conflict that tore my country apart in the past, with the possibility of the Khadri family seizing power.'

'So your father disinherited you to keep the peace,' she said, leaning forward to put her glass on the table, propped her elbows on the table and rested her chin on her hands.

The frost had melted but her sympathies were with his father, with Safia. He would have expected nothing else.

'He flew to London and disinherited me because he was furious. I'd been given an international education to prepare me for my duties as a modern ruler, given freedom to enjoy the sports I loved because it brought honour to our country, and I'd repaid him by behaving like a dissolute playboy and was not fit to rule.' His father's words were carved into his heart. 'He banished me to keep the peace.'

She nodded, clearly understanding the difference. 'So what's this deal, Bram?'

'The price of my return to Umm al Basr is marriage to Ahmed Khadri's youngest daughter, Bibi.'

Only the movement of her throat as she swallowed, drawing attention to the glow of candlelight on the cream silk of her neck, betrayed her shock.

'I'm sorry, Bram, but I don't understand your problem.'

'You are remarkably sanguine,' he said. 'I was sure your western sensibilities would be outraged.'

'By an arranged marriage? It's the cultural norm in this part of the world,' she said, 'and at a much earlier age than the average western marriage.' His surprise must have telegraphed itself. 'This is a return to the status quo,' she added. 'A second chance.' Then she frowned. 'What happened to Safia?'

'The contract was for the marriage of the oldest daughter of the Khadri family to the heir to Umm al Basr. When I was disinherited,' he said, 'my brother took my place. He married Safia Khadri.'

Like Ruby telling him that she had changed her name because of a scandal, that her parents were dead, he kept his voice expressionless, shrugged as if it was no big deal. As if he hadn't given a damn about being disinherited, banished…

'I'd ask how she felt about that,' Ruby replied, 'but I don't suppose she had any choice.'

'Feelings did not come into it. They did their duty.'

'Right…' Ruby eased a finger around the neckline of her top, not quite as laid-back about the situation as she would like him to believe. Which suited him perfectly. She took a sip of juice, set the glass down. 'So what has changed?' she asked.

'Changed?'

'Why is Ahmed Khadri, the man who threatened to kill you on sight, willing to give you his youngest daughter?'

'Safia has given my brother three daughters in five years. With the last pregnancy there were complications. Pre-eclampsia. Hamad has been warned to wait a full two years before trying again for a son.'

'So now her father is prepared to forgive you and sacrifice another daughter to the baby factory?' she demanded, her natural instincts as a liberated woman clearly outraged.

'This has nothing to do with forgiveness; this is politics.'

'To think that when I said medieval I was being flippant. Does Bibi have a choice?'

'In theory. In practice, she will obey her father.'

She shook her head in disbelief. 'Do you know her?'

'Her mother died when she was born and both Safia and Bibi were educated with my sisters at the palace. The last time I saw Bibi Khadri she was a brainy twelve-year-old with her heart set on becoming a doctor. She took her university entrance exams a year early and the last I heard she was going to begin her training in September.'

'*What?* When I said sacrifice—'

'You had no idea how close to the truth you were. Being forced to give up her heart's desire and marry a scarred old man to provide her father with a grandson, her country with an heir, has to be as appalling a prospect to her as bedding a seventeen-year-old virgin is to me.'

'Seventeen? But she's a child,' she said, clearly horrified. 'Not that you're old,' she added quickly.

'You are not a teenager, Ruby. I'm twice her age,' he said, amused by her attempt to save his feelings but determined to press the point home.

She looked thoughtful. 'You do know that it's

the man who decides the sex of the infant? If girls run in your family her sacrifice will have been in vain.'

'Good point. I have four older sisters.'

'Four?' Those expressive brows did a little dance. 'Ahmed Khadri might have a long wait to see a grandson.'

'The seas will run dry before I give him one,' he assured her. 'Bibi is going to be part of a modern Umm al Basr where women have rights, are valued as equals, not traded at the whim of men.'

'So you're doing this for her?'

'No, Ruby, I'm doing it for me. Have you any idea what living with an unwilling teenage bride would be like?'

She sat back and as she looked at him he could see the cogs turning in her brain.

'Are you certain that she's unwilling?'

'What are you suggesting?'

'That while she might have wanted to be a doctor at twelve, at seventeen being the wife of the Emir's son might be a lot more appealing. And if she produces a boy in nine months from now I imagine Ahmed Khadri would be applying pressure for you to be restored to the succession.'

'No doubt,' he said. 'Thankfully, Bibi, who is already in pre-wedding seclusion, managed to smuggle a note to her sister. A plea for help. Until that moment no one but my father and Ahmed Khadri knew of the plan.'

'Your brother warned you?' He nodded. 'But if you arrive with a wife surely it will be back to square one?'

'A secret works two ways. On the one hand I return home to be presented with a *fait accompli* in which the consequences of my refusal to accept Bibi as my bride would be catastrophic. On the other I arrive, totally unaware of what has been planned, with a brand-new wife to present to my family. What can anyone say?'

'Quite a lot, I imagine.'

'No doubt, but none of it out loud. My father is a politician. He will hide his pleasure at besting an old enemy. As for Ahmed Khadri, he has nothing to gain from creating a crisis. No doubt he extracted an eye-watering dowry from my father in return for giving his youngest daughter to a disgraced son. More than enough to cover the expense of setting up and running a house for Bibi in England while she studies medicine.'

'So everyone will be satisfied.'

'You don't sound convinced.'

With the slightest movement of her head she said, 'I was wondering what will happen a few weeks down the line when you announce the marriage is over.'

'Everyone will think I've been a fool?' he suggested. 'Nothing new there.'

'Everyone will think it was very convenient.'

'Point taken.' He hadn't thought much beyond the immediate problem. Beyond this week. 'What is the longest you've ever temped for anyone?'

'Six months. To cover maternity leave.' She lifted elegant shoulders in the briefest of shrugs. 'It was my first temporary job. A one-man office.'

Six months… What would it be like to have Ruby Dance at his side for six months? Sparky, smart-mouthed. Those extraordinary grey eyes full of questions…

'Did you enjoy it?' he asked.

'He was patient, very kind at a bad time for me. I still temp for him when he needs someone.' The implication being that while she was now in demand from those at the top of the business tree, she did not forget those who'd helped her.

'I'm neither patient nor kind,' he said, 'but if you will give me six months of your time I will make it worth your while.'

'Is there no one else you could ask?' she said. 'A friend?'

'Time is short, you are here and a straightforward business arrangement will be simpler.' He met her direct gaze head-on. 'How much is six months of your life worth, Ruby?' he asked. 'Name your price.'

Ruby froze. Until this moment his proposition had felt rhetorical but suddenly it was very real and her first reaction was *No way*. Deception of any kind was abhorrent to her but this was different. She would be hurting no one. On the contrary, she would be reuniting Bram with his father, saving a very young woman from a forced marriage—both noble aims.

And he'd asked her to name her price. It wasn't an idle offer. He was a billionaire and the sum in her head would be peanuts to him while to her it would mean a new start, a chance to clear the last of her father's debts, wipe the slate clean, be free…

'I need to think,' she said. 'I need to walk. Is the beach safe?' she said, standing up.

'Walking at night by yourself is not wise,' he said, rising to join her, apparently able to read her mind. 'I go to the stables when I need to think through a difficult decision. Horses make great listeners.'

She swallowed down the sudden lump in her throat, remembering the hours she'd spent talking to her horses as she'd brushed their coats. The confidences she'd shared with them. Her ambitions, her first crush, her first kiss…

'Would you like to come and meet them?' he asked.

No... Yes... She looked at her barely touched plate. 'Will you apologise to Mina for me?'

'Of course.'

He paused to speak to Mina and then led the way across the terrace and down more steps that led to a large courtyard sheltered by the rear of the fort.

Concealed lighting, activated by movement, flickered on around the yard and for a moment she paused to breathe in the familiar scent of hay and warm horseflesh as Bram disappeared into the tack room and returned with a handful of carrots.

There was a soft whicker from the first horse-box and then the pale grey head of a magnificent horse appeared over the half door and reached towards Bram.

He murmured soft words in Arabic as he rubbed his hand down the dished face before turning to her. 'This is Vega. The brightest of my stars.'

'*Salaam*, Vega.' She approached him carefully, as she would any unknown animal, offering her hand to be sniffed at and, when that was approved, offering him the carrot that Bram handed to her.

The horse lipped it from her palm, allowing her to rub his nose as he crunched it.

Bram led the way around the yard, introducing her to his beautiful horses, saying nothing as she greeted each one, was accepted, allowed to run a hand down a warm neck, fondle an ear, stroke a cheek.

'They are all so beautiful, Bram,' she said with a sigh.

'Who do you think would make the best listener?'

'Rigel,' she said, without hesitation. A silky chestnut with a black mane and a white blaze on his forehead who had pushed his head towards her, laying his forehead against her shoulder.

Without another word, Bram fetched a body brush from the tack room, handed it to her and opened the door to Rigel's stable. 'Get to know one another. Take as long as you need. I'll be with my hawks.'

Bram was smiling as he walked across to the mews. He'd seen her hesitation when he'd invited her to ride, the longing in her eyes even as she'd shaken her head, made a joke about keeping out of danger.

Any doubts he might have had were banished the moment Rigel, the most intuitive of his horses, had pushed his head into her shoulder. From across the yard he could hear her voice, silky soft, as she brushed him down, coming to her decision.

Ruby did not need time. She had seen the man with his horses, the way they reached to him, almost purred at his touch, and her decision was made. But this closeness with a horse, once so much part of her life, this was a pleasure she would not surrender. She laid her hand against Rigel's neck and he turned to look at her, gave her a nudge as if to say, *What are you waiting for?*

Half an hour later, having returned the brush to the tack room and washed her hands, Ruby found Bram in his mews.

He returned the hawk on his fist to its perch, removed his glove. 'All done?' he said, joining her in the yard.

'I have a question,' she said.

'Just one?'

'Just one.'

'Go ahead.'

'If I said no, what would you do?'

The moon had risen, silvering her hair…

'Bram?'

He shook off the thought. A straightforward business transaction. It had to be that.

'I wish to see my father, receive his blessing more than anything in the world, Ruby, but not at any price. If you say no, then I will send my father my good wishes for his birthday, as I do every year, and my regret that I cannot be there to celebrate the day with him.'

He saw her throat move as she swallowed, took a breath. 'Six months?'

'It's a great deal to ask.'

'It's just a job,' she reminded him.

'Yes.' Silvering her hair, her cheek, her mouth—

'I don't know anything about marriage laws in this part of the world,' she said, cutting off the thought before he could put it into words. 'Can it be arranged in the time?'

'Practical as ever.'

'And?'

The simple answer, the practical answer, was yes. Right at that moment, standing in the moonlight, he was feeling anything but practical.

'Under normal circumstances there would be months of negotiation over the dowry.'

'Months?'

'A man's sons are his future but his daughters are his wealth. That's why they're so carefully protected.'

'Oh, I see. Well, we don't have months to haggle but that's not a problem. What I'm asking for is not up for negotiation.'

'I'm listening.'

'One—you will pay Amanda for my services as your temp while I'm here. I will need something to do, you will still need a PA and she's going to have to reschedule all my bookings so she's entitled to her fee.'

'That is eminently reasonable.'

'Two—you will pay a lump sum, clear of tax, to my lawyer at the end of this engagement as a bonus.' The amount she named was not a round sum, but down to the last odd pence.

He would have gladly given her four times that, but clearly there was a reason for that odd amount and now was not the time to argue. 'Consider it done. Go on.'

'Go on?'

'Three?'

'There isn't a three.' She gave him an odd little smile. Bright on the surface but suspiciously close to tears underneath. 'So,' she said, as they returned to the terrace and their abandoned supper. 'That's the dowry taken care of. What comes next?'

Mina arrived, clucking and worrying. He'd explained that Ruby was feeling tired after her journey and now she'd brought mint tea, dates, nuts, little sweet pastries.

He assured her that he would see she ate something and, reluctantly, she left them to it.

'Next,' he said, pouring the tea, 'you eat something or I'll be in trouble with Mina.'

'What comes next in the wedding arrangements?' she asked, taking a date.

'Next, you would go into seclusion for weeks, seeing no one outside the women in your immediate family until the *maksar*. That's a gathering where the entire Ansari tribe come to check out the dowry and eat themselves sick for days. No one will expect that with a disinherited son and a western bride.'

The corner of her mouth tilted up, revealing a dimple. 'Shame. It sounds like quite a party.'

'But not one that the bride takes part in. She stays hidden away until her groom fights his way through her family to claim her.'

'He has to fight his way through?' she asked. 'Despite the dowry?'

He found himself hesitating as an old image flooded his mind. The anticipation of the mock battle as he fought his way past her brothers. Safia swathed in veils that he would remove one by one…

He shook his head. 'All of which is irrelevant in our case. I'll call my cousin and ask him to draw up a contract. I could do it myself but the seal of the Emir of Ras al Kawi will lend it legitimacy. We will formalise the arrangement tomorrow before the charity dinner.'

'I hate to break this to you, Bram, but you're going to need more than a contract to convince your family that this is a genuine marriage.'

'A contract is hard to ignore,' Bram pointed out.

'I agree, but this isn't an arranged marriage with every detail hammered out by families who have known one another for generations. I can't speak for the men, but the women in your family will want all the details. The when, where and how we met. How we got from there to here. We're going to need a story.'

Bram rubbed a hand over his face. 'I thought this was going to be simple.'

'It will be,' she assured him. 'All it requires is a little preparation so that we get the basics straight.' She took another date. 'Let's start with how we met. London seems the most likely place.'

He shrugged. 'I was there for a week last December.'

She shook her head. 'That's too recent. How often do you go to London?'

'It varies. About once a month, more often when a new project is kicking off.'

'Do you take Peter with you?'

'He usually takes advantage of my absence to go into the desert with his camera.' Then, catching her meaning, 'I suppose, if I needed someone, he could ask his godmother to provide a PA.'

'That seems likely and, naturally, she would have sent her very best.'

'Naturally.'

'And you were so impressed—'

'—that I always asked for you when I was in London.'

'Anyone would,' she assured him and he rewarded her with a smile for her cheek. 'Obviously, when Peter called asking her to send someone to cover for him, she would have asked me to drop everything and fly to Ras al Kawi.'

'Obviously.' His grin faded. 'And that first moment, when I saw you—'

'—you realised that you couldn't live without me.'

For a moment they just stared at one another as the whisper of a breeze caught the flame of the candle and sent it dancing, throwing shadows up the walls.

'Well, that's a great start but we're going to need more than that.'

'Are we?'

Ruby firmly suppressed a little shiver that ran up her spine. It was getting chilly.

'Me,' she said. 'I'm going to need more. You'll probably just get a blokeish slap on the back, but the women in your family—your mother, your sisters—will give me the full who-the-heck-are-you-and-what-makes-you-think-you're-good-enough-for-our-boy? interrogation.'

Amused, he said, 'I didn't realise you'd met them.'

'Mothers, sisters, are the same the world over, Bram, and once they've sorted out the how and where they'll want every detail of how we got from personal assistant to personal.'

His smile faded.

He clearly hadn't thought this through before

he'd asked for her help. He'd been solely focused on protecting Bibi Khadri from her father's machinations and was only now beginning to realise the extent of what he'd taken on. Or, more realistically, what she'd taken on, because men didn't do personal stuff. She was the one who would be facing the in-depth interrogation.

'Will you be able to handle that?' he asked.

'Yes,' she said, 'but we will need to have our stories straight.'

Neither of them spoke for a moment, then Bram said, 'Okay, keeping it real…I could have kept you late one night and then insisted on taking you out to dinner.'

'To thank me for all my hard work?'

'Maybe I was being selfish,' he said, a smile tugging at the corner of his lip. 'I didn't want to eat alone and you are an intelligent and attractive woman.'

It was ridiculous to blush. He said attractive, not beautiful, and they were creating a legend, a story. A lie.

'You eat alone?' she asked, ignoring the little cold spot at her core. The realisation that she was inventing a history, just as her father had done a hundred times or more. And so easily…

In a good cause, she told herself. In a good cause.

'My life has changed,' Bram said, distracting

her. 'I no longer move in the same circles as I did when I lived in Europe.'

He was lonely?

No, no...

Stick to the details. Working late. Dinner… It could have happened exactly like that. She'd had the invitations, but had always said no…

'Right, well, that's real enough,' she said briskly. 'So, where did you take me?'

He thought about it for a moment before naming a selection of the most exclusive and expensive restaurants currently fashionable in the city.

'Bram Ansari, you are the kind of boss I've always dreamed of,' she said, 'but I would have been working for ten hours and would have needed a shower and change of clothes for anywhere that special.'

'The shower I could arrange…' He cleared his throat. 'Perhaps not. Besides, it was late and there was no way I could have got a table. My gratitude would have had to wait until the following evening.'

'You were leaving the following day,' she reminded him.

'I was?'

'Your plane was waiting at London City Airport, the flight plan filed. And neither of us had eaten since I shared my packed lunch with you at lunchtime.'

He looked at her for a moment and then, unexpectedly, he laughed. 'You're really getting into this.'

Of course she was. She was a con man's daughter and the apple didn't fall far from the tree but she wasn't hurting anyone, cheating anyone…

'I'm the go-to woman for detail,' she said.

'Okay, so it's late, we're tired and hungry. What do you suggest?'

'A quick trip to the nearest fast food outlet?' she offered, mentally waving goodbye to the Michelin stars. 'Or we could have ordered in a Chinese. Where would we have been? You don't have an office in London.'

'I have a service flat at the Savoy,' he said. 'I work from there.'

Okaaay... 'Well, no problem. Obviously, you called up room service. I would have been happy with scrambled egg and a pot of tea but you insisted on a proper meal and champagne because one of the ventures you'd financed had just been launched on the Stock Exchange…' She snapped out of her story. 'Do you drink champagne?'

'It has been known,' he said wryly.

'Oh, yes…' Colour rose to her cheeks as she recalled the photographs of him in that fountain, naked, his arm around a girl who had stripped down to transparently wet underwear, his mouth open as he'd poured champagne over them both.

She cleared her throat. 'So let's say this happened about eighteen months ago. That would have been about the time of the Maxim Sports flotation.'

'How would you know that?' he asked, losing the smile.

'It's not a secret.'

'I'm not suggesting that it is. I'm asking how you know that off the top of your head,' he persisted. 'Please don't tell me that you read up on it on your way here.'

She swallowed, wishing she'd kept her smart mouth shut instead of getting carried away with their story. Too late and now he'd gone all suspicious on her. She would never tell him the truth—that she'd hoped to recoup a large amount, at least large enough to finally settle her father's debt. She wouldn't have seen a penny of that money for herself.

'I know,' she said, 'because I invested some of my hard-earned in the launch shares.'

'You play the market?' he asked with an edge in his voice sharp enough to cut steel.

'I don't play at anything.' She had done nothing wrong and yet all her instincts had instantly gone on the defensive. As had his. There was no smile now, none of the warmth that a moment ago had fed their game, only suspicion as she was forced onto the back foot, having to justify what she did. 'That six-month maternity cover was for a stockbroker. I've learned a lot from him over the years, including the advice to follow a smart venture capitalist by the name of Bram Ansari.'

'No doubt. And I imagine that as you go from company to company you pick up a great deal of privileged information,' he said, ignoring her last comment, 'which you feed back to him.'

On the word of a friend, the assurance of a young man who'd never met her, he had confided in her, laid himself bare, hostage to her discretion. With one careless remark she had shattered that trust. She didn't answer but reached into her bag for her tablet, calling on every ounce of self-control to keep her hands steady as she pulled up a folder.

'That's my portfolio. If you check it against my work diary you'll see that I've never invested in any of the companies I've worked for.' She stood up, placed it in front of him and turned to leave but he caught her hand.

'Ruby…'

'It's all there. Dates, amounts, profits…'

'Sit down.'

When she didn't move he looked up, his golden eyes gleaming in the light of the candles.

'Will you please sit down, Ruby?'

She lowered herself to the edge of the chair but he still kept his hand lightly wrapped around hers as he flicked through her trading history. He wasn't restraining her, simply holding her hand. She could have pulled away. She should have pulled away—

'You had funds from the sale of the Maxim shares but you didn't invest in Oliver Brent's venture,' he said after a while.

'No.'

He looked up. 'Was there any special reason for that?'

'Nothing that would make sense to you.'

'Try me.'

'It was nothing.' Bram Ansari simply waited. 'He had a smile that could sell false teeth to a shark.' She lifted her shoulders a millimetre or two. 'I'm sure Oliver Brent is solid as a rock. Shares in his company have gone through the roof in the last twelve months. My mistake,' she added.

'No.' He released her hand, sat back in his chair, putting a little distance between them so that she could breathe again. 'You have to trust your instincts. If your gut tells you to walk away, no matter how good it looks, then that's the right decision.'

He looked up, met her gaze then closed her tablet and handed it back to her.

'An interesting portfolio but you take your profit too soon.'

'I have expenses.'

He nodded. 'Take a look at the pitches in my

pending file when you have time. I'd be interested to know if anything catches your eye.'

He hadn't apologised for jumping to the wrong conclusion, accusing her of insider trading, but she had been given something infinitely more precious. His trust.

'So tell me, Ruby, what did we eat that first night?'

She blinked at the abrupt change of subject, taking a moment to catch up. 'Eat? I don't know. I'll have to check the Savoy's menu online.'

'They will prepare anything at the Grill but there is a great seafood bar.' He glanced up and his eyes glowed amber in the candlelight. 'Do you enjoy shellfish?'

'Yes,' she said quickly. 'Yes, I love it.'

'Then maybe we'd have started with a shared platter. Oysters, lobster tails, smoked salmon?'

The night was still, black and warm around them. The only sounds were the soft swoosh of the sea lapping against the sand in the cove below them, a cicada warming up in fits and starts. They were alone in the small circle of candlelight and for a moment the beginning of this make-believe love affair felt real. She could imagine them sitting over supper, talking, just like they were tonight.

'D-delicious,' she said, her voice thick.

'What next? Will you stay with fish or they do a very fine burger?'

'We were talking,' she said. 'I didn't notice what we had next except there was something out of this world made of chocolate for dessert and the richest coffee I've ever tasted.'

'Oh?' He propped his elbows on the table and rested his chin on his hands, smiling now. 'What were we talking about that was so distracting?'

'I asked you about the company you were about to invest in, why them…'

'Eighteen months ago?' He thought about it for a moment. 'That would have to be Shadbrook. It's still early days.'

'I read something about them last week,' she said. 'Eco-energy?' And, just like that, they were off and talking about the company, the passion of the people involved, and she didn't notice that she'd demolished the dish of fruit and sweets that Mina had brought them.

Eventually she ran out of questions and they fell silent.

'And then, Ruby?' he said softly, looking at her intently. 'When we stopped talking what did we do then?'

'I…' For a moment it had been so real, almost as if they were back in London eighteen months ago, eating fabulous food, talking about something that fascinated them both. 'It was late,' she said. 'You called for your car and sent me home in style.'

'And immediately cancelled my flight to New York so that I could see you the next day.'

'No…I wouldn't have been free. You were lucky to have had me for a day.'

'Ruby, Ruby…' He laughed softly. 'Okay, so I had to leave the next day but my driver had your address,' he said, his voice like silk velvet against her skin. 'I would have been on your doorstep as the sun rose with coffee and warm *pain au chocolat* so that we could have breakfast together.'

The image he'd painted was so real that she could see herself rushing to the door in her bathrobe, imagining her elderly neighbour had some problem. Opening it to find Bram Ansari filling her doorway, a glossy paper carrier from some smart bakery in his hand, his tawny eyes hungry for more than pastry.

'Yes…' The word was little more than a breath.

For a moment neither of them moved.

'You've had a long day,' Bram said, abruptly pushing his chair back and standing up. 'We'll continue this in the morning.'

She swallowed, forced herself to focus on the reality not the dream.

'Long and unusual,' she agreed as he held her chair so that she could get to her feet. From doubting that Bram Ansari would accept her as his PA, she was now going to be his wife. It might be no more than a paper marriage but she still needed to process the situation, make a plan, think herself into the role and become a woman his family would believe he loved.

There were a dozen details they needed to hammer out but she needed a little space to think it through and, slipping her tablet back into her bag, she rose to her feet.

She was tall but he was half a head taller. As she turned from the table she found herself staring at the scar beneath his left eye and, without thinking, she reached up, her fingers a hair's breadth from touching him.

'I dishonoured Safia Khadri. Someone who loved her thought I should have a permanent reminder.'

'You could have lost an eye.'

'He was too angry to care,' he said, reaching up, taking the hand hovering over the scar and, still holding it, headed for the steps, walking her up to her suite as if they were really that couple who, lost to reality, had shared breakfast in bed in her tiny flat before he'd flown away. Who had snatched precious moments whenever he'd passed through London.

Who had looked at one another this evening and realised that they could no longer live without one another.

They were creating a legend but that was not enough. They were going to have to put on a convincing performance as newlyweds, appear to all the world as if they couldn't keep their hands off one another.

It was just part of the job, she told herself as he glanced back to make sure she was managing the oldest, narrowest and most uneven part of the steps. The place where she'd stumbled on the way down and he'd held her and for a moment she'd forgotten everything she'd learned about the danger of getting close to someone. The risk of hurting not just herself, because that didn't matter, but some innocent who deserved more.

Briefly forgotten and just as quickly recovered.

This was a business arrangement first, last and everything in between. Bram couldn't have asked her to go through with a paper marriage if it had been anything more.

She could not have accepted.

'Have you thought about a gift for your father?' she asked, retrieving her hand as they reached her level, determined to focus on her job.

'I've been training a young falcon.' He was looking to the south, to Umm al Basr, and for a moment his guard was down and the longing to be home was painfully exposed.

'I'm sure he'll appreciate the personal nature of such a gift,' she said.

'I hope so.'

'He made a deal with an old enemy because he wants you near him,' she said softly. 'He won't send you away again.'

He turned to look at her and for a moment it took all her willpower not to put her arms around him, hold him. Then he shook his head and all trace of vulnerability vanished.

'Give me your phone. I need your number. And the name of your lawyer.'

'Do you need it now?'

'Please.'

'I'll text their details to you.'

'What about Amanda?' he asked as he sent the numbers to his own phone.

'She'll invoice you.'

'Will you tell her why you're staying on?'

'Oh, yes, I suppose so. There's bound to be publicity. Errant son arrives home with unsuitable bride is a story made for *Celebrity*.'

'Not in Umm al Basr. Family matters are private. Wives are very private.'

'In this day and age? You were an internationally famous sportsman. Front cover material.'

'No one who values the good opinion of the Emir will be phoning in this story,' he assured her. 'Despite all the publicity when I was disinherited, Safia's name was never mentioned.'

'Well, good.' She managed a grin. 'It will make

returning to work when this is all over a great deal easier.'

She'd changed her name and the chances of anyone seeing her photograph and connecting it with a slightly tubby sixteen-year-old astride a horse were vanishingly small but even so his confidence was reassuring.

'In fact, the fewer people who know the better. I'll simply tell her you've asked me to stay until Peter returns.' She nodded towards the phone he was holding. 'I should have your number too.'

'It's done,' he said, handing it back to her. 'You'll be getting a call from Princess Violet's assistant, Leila Darwish, within the hour. She'll want your measurements, shoe size.'

'Oh, but—'

'You will need more than a boring black dress if you're going to convince anyone that you're my wife.'

'Really?' she replied, back in PA mode. 'I fly in out of the blue, we fall into one another's arms and twenty-four hours later you present me to your father as your new wife. Do you really think we'd have wasted much time worrying about what I was going to wear, let alone going on a major shopping spree?'

'I…' He shook his head, clearly not prepared to go there. 'No.'

'And your sisters will have less time to cross-question me if they're distracted by the task of helping me shop for a wardrobe fit for a princess.'

'They are going to love you, Ruby.'

'But not too much. You'll want their sympathy, not their blame when it's over. I may have to let being a princess go to my head. Become a bit of a diva.'

He shook his head. 'Peter was right. You are very good.'

CHAPTER FOUR

RUBY CLOSED THE door and leaned back against it, heart pounding, mouth dry. A princessy diva? She'd spent the last ten years living below the radar, being invisible. How on earth was she going to pull that off?

It had seemed so simple when Bram had put the proposition to her. No more than a little extra twist on the job. But it wasn't going to be that easy. His family would be suspicious—any family would be suspicious—and there were a dozen questions she should have asked.

Where would they stay in Umm al Basr? And if it was in the palace, how would they handle the sleeping arrangements?

And that was before she got into the whole major wardrobe makeover. Her limited wardrobe of classics in a grey/black palette wouldn't take her past day one and, much as she hated the idea of having clothes bought for her, it was obvious that she'd need clothes to support the story.

Princess Violet's mouth-watering designs had made a big impact when they'd been launched at London Fashion Week and she was woman enough to want to appear at the palace wearing something stunning, if only to give her the poise she'd need to carry this off.

And if she blasted into the palace full of confidence and with a knock-out wardrobe, his female relatives would take an instant dislike to her. Uncomfortable, but for the best.

Bram was not about to embarrass his cousin by asking him to collude in this paper marriage and was relieved to find that his quick sketch of the story Ruby had woven around their 'romance' had been accepted without the least suspicion.

'This is wonderful news, my friend. You've been alone for too long,' Fayad said, clearly delighted. 'Does Ruby have family to negotiate for her?'

'No, she is quite alone. Will you stand for her in the question of the contract?'

'It will be my pleasure. There's not much time so we should begin.'

Fayad was as meticulous as if he'd been negotiating for his own daughter but finally it was done and arrangements made for the signing ceremony before the charity dinner the following evening.

Ask the Garland Girl, Peter had said and, in desperation, he'd asked the impossible of Ruby Dance. He could hardly believe that she'd said yes. He should have insisted that she sleep on her decision. He should call her now and tell her that she must do that.

He picked up his phone but, with his thumb poised over the call button, he pulled back. She'd do that anyway and he wouldn't have to ask her on which side her decision had landed when he saw her tomorrow morning. She might have a face made for poker but he'd know the moment he set eyes on her if she'd changed her mind.

Meanwhile, there were things he needed to do, to have in place, in case she was prepared to go ahead.

Ruby knew that she would not sleep until she had her head straight around all the questions that seemed to spring into her mind the moment she was alone. She explored the little kitchen and made herself a cup of tea before settling down with a notebook and pen and began making a list.

She wasn't clear whether he had been completely cut off from his family. He appeared to be in touch with his brother, but what about the rest of the family? Did he meet them in London? Did they visit him here in Ras al Kawi? Would he have talked to her about them, or would such a relationship have been off the conversational agenda? And how should she address his mother, for instance? And his father, assuming things went well enough for her to meet him.

And there were a hundred other things.

What was his favourite food? What music did he enjoy? What would he have shared with her about his childhood? Those were the details that would help her convince a sceptical mother or sister that their relationship was real.

And the really big one, the elephant in the room, where were they going to sleep?

There wasn't going to be a lot of time tomorrow and she texted him her questions so that he would have time to think about it and have his answers ready.

That done, she laid out the clothes she would wear to travel in, checked over the dress and bolero jacket she would wear for the dinner at the palace in Ras al Kawi and then ran a bath. She was about to step into it when her phone pinged.

She picked it up and smiled as she saw that Bram had responded.

My sisters are Almira, Hasna, Fathia and Nadiya. I'll give you a list of their children and their accomplishments in the morning. Music? A mixed bag from rock to classical. Where do you live, Ruby?

She sank into the bath and texted back.

Good point. Camden.

She added the address.

Up the first flight of stairs and on the right. Tiny hall, sitting room on the left, bedroom on the right, bathroom, minute kitchen. 'Stairway to Heaven'?

She added a smiley and clicked 'send'.

A moment or two later the guitar solo at the opening of the track rippled softly from an unseen speaker and she sank lower into the bath, closing her eyes as the song built and the lyrics filled her head. There was a line in there somewhere about looking to the west. Was he torn, she wondered, between his longing for home and his old life in Europe? The rush of downhill racing, the polo matches, the aristocratic groupies…

A beep recalled her to their conversation.

What do you drive?

In London? Are you kidding? A bike.

With a basket on the front?

Is there any other kind? she replied, smiling now. What's your comfort food?

Comfort food?

The only thing you want when you've been dumped…

Although she doubted that had ever happened to him.

Or have man flu, or your team lost the big match.

Her thumbs were flying over the letters.

Tinned tomato soup? A fried egg sandwich? A cheeseburger?

I'll go with the burger.

With pickles?

With extra pickles. What's your favourite colour? No, don't tell me—dark ruby-red.

Before she could reply, the phone rang.

'Whoah!' she said.

'Did I startle you?'

'I nearly dropped the phone in the bath.'

There was silence from the other end of the phone and she bit her lower lip. Stupid thing to say…

'Do you have speakers in every room in the house?' she asked quickly.

'Each apartment is individually Internet enabled. You can download anything your mood dictates.'

'Impressive. What are you listening to?'

'You,' he said. 'I'm listening to you. No, I'm talking to you. Are you quite sure about this, Ruby?'

'Quite sure,' she said, touched that he was concerned about her when this meant so much to him. He could have no idea how much it meant to her. Freedom… 'This is a temporary assignment like any other but there are a few details we have to sort out.'

'Be certain,' he warned, 'because the moment the contract is signed you will be Princess Ruby of Umm al Basr.'

She swallowed. She was kidding herself; this wasn't like any other temp placement she'd had. Not at all.

'That will be weird.'

'It's just a form of address. Like Miss. Or Mrs.'

Of course it was…

'I'll try and remember that.' Back to the list. 'Do you see any of your family?'

'Occasionally. When my mother and sisters are in London.'

'Your brother?'

'We keep in touch. I saw him when my father had his heart bypass operation in London last year.'

About to ask if he had seen his father then, she thought better of it. He would have said he'd seen his brother when he was visiting his father. Clearly, banishment meant more than exile from his country.

The water was tepid when she finally climbed out of the bath, wrapped herself in the fluffy robe hanging behind the door and curled up with her notebook, writing down everything he'd told her about his family, his life.

It was barely light when Bram mounted Antares and rode him hard into the dawn. Last night everything had seemed so simple but in the light of dawn he knew that where emotions ran high nothing was certain.

He paused at the top of a low promontory looking down the Gulf towards the Indian Ocean and, for just a moment, wondered what it would be like to have Ruby beside him astride Rigel, witnessing the sunrise, watching the shadows shrink…

He headed for the kitchen, planning to grab a cup of coffee, take a shower then find Ruby and offer her a last chance to change her mind. Ruby was ahead of him.

She was sitting at the breakfast counter, long legs twined around the stool, a fork halfway to her lips, laughing at something that Mina was saying more with actions than words.

He leaned over and helped himself to a piece of the pineapple she was eating. She turned and looked up at him, her lips a startled O, gleaming with sweet juice…

'*Aasif,*' he apologised as Mina muttered disapprovingly. 'I've brought the smell of the stables into her kitchen.'

'It's a good smell. It takes me back…'

She broke off, but she didn't need to explain. Scent was the most evocative of the senses and it was obvious last night that she had spent a great deal of time around horses before whatever scandal had blighted her family. Before the death of her parents.

No ties.

Like him, she was not so much unattached as detached.

'I saw last night how good you were with the horses. Rigel would never let just anyone take a brush to him.' He poured himself a glass of juice. 'You were one of those horse-mad little girls,' he said, resisting the temptation to lay his hand on her shoulder so that she would know she was not alone. 'A member of the Pony Club. Bouncing around on a little pony.'

She didn't say anything but the answer was in her eyes. The painful glow of a passion that could never be entirely extinguished. The memory of horses that had become a part of her.

'When we return to the fort we'll ride together.'

She shook her head, stiff now. 'No. I told you. I don't ride. Thank you.'

'Did you have a fall?' he asked.

'No…' She pulled a face, made an effort to smile that was painful to watch. 'Well, yes, obviously, dozens of them, but it's not that.'

Ruby's mouth was dry. She would have picked up the glass of juice Mina had poured for her but her hand would shake so much she'd spill it.

Last night she'd felt the soft lips of a horse taking a carrot from her hand, she'd run a hand over its neck, remembered the exhilaration as half a ton of the most beautiful animal on earth lifted her over a fence. Riding was something that had happened in another life—one that she'd lost on the day when her world had fallen apart.

She could ride here on one of Bram's fine horses—was already half in love with Rigel. But when she returned to London, to reality, she would lose it all over again.

Aware that he was waiting for some explanation, she fell back on her original excuse. 'You'll recall that I'm under strict orders from Amanda not to take part in any dangerous sports while I'm here.'

'And yet you agreed to marry me.'

'Marriage isn't a sport.' The heat coming off him might be warming her, the scent of fresh sweat, horse flesh, warm leather making her feel slightly dizzy, but they had laid down the ground rules and any danger was entirely in her head. 'In this case it's not even a marriage.'

'Just an extension of your role as my personal assistant.' He didn't say the words that they were thinking—no sex—but his smile was little more than a twist of his lips. 'With the fewer people who know about it the better.'

Confused by his irritation—surely he must want the same thing—she said, 'What about Khal? He knows that you hadn't met me before today.'

'Khal will keep his thoughts to himself.'

'And Mina? How will she take the news?'

'Shall we find out?' he asked as she returned with his coffee.

Her response was to let out a scream, put her hands to her face as she poured forth a stream of joyful congratulations. Then she flung her arms around him, kissed him on both cheeks before grabbing Ruby and repeating the performance, almost bouncing on the spot before rushing off to share the news with the rest of her family.

'Does that answer your question?' he asked with a wry smile, clearly expecting her to be amused. He couldn't have been more wrong.

'She thinks you're happy,' she said, horrified. As would his mother, his sisters…

'I am,' he assured her. 'Tomorrow, thanks to you, I will be home for the first time in five years.' He picked up his cup and made a move. 'Eat your breakfast, Ruby. It's going to be a long day.'

'It's going to be a long day for both of us but Mina will think it odd if you rush away.' She offered him a piece of pineapple on a fork. 'We need to talk.'

'Those details you wanted to sort out?' He ignored the pineapple but slid onto the stool beside her. 'I imagine you're concerned about sleeping arrangements.'

She felt her cheeks heat up. Which was ridiculous.

'We'll take the boat down to Umm al Basr and stay on board while we're there,' he said, cutting her off before she could get the wrong idea. 'It has a communications centre—there are those video conferences, phone calls—and we'll have our own living space and staff, which will cut out the palace gossip,' he added, lifting his head as he heard the helicopter approaching. 'How soon can you be ready to leave?'

Ruby had just zipped up her case when her phone rang. She looked at the caller ID and said, 'Hi, Amanda.'

'Is this a good time?'

'Not really. We're leaving for the capital very

shortly. Princess Violet is holding a charity dinner this evening.'

'Then I won't keep you. I just need to know how long you'll be staying. If it's more than a week I'll need to rearrange your schedule.'

'Bram wants me to stay until Peter is well enough to return,' she replied, fudging it.

'Bram? When you called yesterday I had the feeling things were not going that well.'

Oh...sherbet dabs.

'My arrival came as a complete surprise. Communication failure,' she said. 'Once he'd spoken to Jude Radcliffe and Peter he was fine.'

'First name terms, fine?'

'Everyone is on first name terms here.'

'Oh, right. Are you happy to stay that long? According to Elizabeth, it's likely to be a few months before Peter's back on his feet.'

'If it's not a problem?' She hated letting down people who were expecting her but, while there were plenty of well qualified staff on Amanda's books to cover for her, there was no one else who could be the temp that Bram needed right now.

'Yes, but it's mine, not yours. I knew the situation when I sent you to Ras al Kawi. I'll keep an eye on your flat while you're away. Do you want me to forward your mail?'

'Don't bother. It will be nothing but junk mail

and bills and they're paid by direct debit. I have to go, Amanda. I'll give you a call later in the week.'

Ruby and Bram were met at the helipad by a car that took them into the heart of the palace complex. When it came to a halt, Bram helped her out but left the car door open.

'You're not staying?' she asked as he made a move to get back in the car.

'Fayad is expecting me. Go and enjoy yourself.'

'Enjoy myself?'

He smiled. 'I'll come and fetch you when everything is ready.' With that, he climbed back into the car and she watched as he was driven away.

For all her outward confidence, all her experience at the high end of business, nothing had prepared her for this. It was one thing to agree to be a pretend bride but, despite the easy banter as they'd built the story of their meeting, the comfortable way they'd shared breakfast with Mina fussing around them, she was about to marry a total stranger and she was a bundle of nerves. As she'd lain awake in the unaccustomed darkness, silence—missing the background sound of a great city to lull her to sleep—her mind had conjured up a dozen reasons why it was not going to work.

'Miss Dance?' She turned to find an elegant young woman walking towards her, hand outstretched. 'Welcome to the palace, Miss Dance. I'm Leila Darwish, Princess Violet's assistant.'

She took her hand. 'Please, call me Ruby.'

'If you'll come this way?'

Ruby followed her through the ornately decorated arch, across a courtyard where water burbled softly over smooth rocks, cooling the air, and on into the interior of a reception room large enough to throw a serious party.

Waiting there was a woman of about her own height, dark hair falling nearly to her waist. She was wearing a soft silk *salwar kameez* in a stunning mix of violet and a rare turquoise green that exactly matched the colour of her eyes.

With a wide smile she took her hands, kissed both her cheeks and said, 'Welcome, Ruby. I'm so glad that Bram has found someone to share his life.' Despite a serious nose that betrayed the Arab genes handed down from her great-grandmother, Princess Violet retained a touch of the streets of London in her accent. 'I've always thought how lonely he must be out at the fort.'

'Th-thank you, Princess—' she managed, stunned that the Ruler's wife had taken time to meet her when she had to be busy putting the finishing touches to her charity dinner. Or maybe a princess had people to do that for her.

'Violet,' she urged. 'By this evening we will be cousins. Fayad and I are so happy that the Emir has called Bram home. It's such an important moment and made even more special by the fact that he can take the woman he loves home with him.'

'I…' Speechless, she fell back on the only thing she could say. 'Thank you.'

'Let's have tea while we talk clothes.'

'Clothes?'

'Bram spoke to Fayad last night and asked if I'd help you sort out your trousseau. His mother and sisters will want to see everything and his instructions were to ensure that they drool with envy.'

'Oh, but…' He'd totally ignored her suggestion that his sister should have that pleasure. Or maybe he'd listened when she'd said that they shouldn't love her. 'That's what he meant when he said to enjoy myself?' she asked.

Violet laughed. 'Undoubtedly, and we will, but first we have to find something for you to wear for the ceremony. I don't imagine you packed a just-in-case wedding dress?' she teased.

'Um, no… Just my work wardrobe. I'm a bit shell-shocked at the speed of this, to be honest,' Ruby said, making an effort to get with the narrative.

'I know the feeling. Fayad took me by surprise too. If I hadn't had Leila to guide me through the minefield of palace etiquette I don't know what I would have done. She is the sister of my soul.'

The two women exchanged a look of such fondness that Ruby felt a pang of loneliness. She was close to Amanda but this was clearly something very special.

'I envy you,' she said. 'I longed for a sister.' And then, when her world imploded, had been glad that there was no one else to be hurt.

'Bram said you have no family.'

Clearly he'd done everything he could to make this easy for her and she shook her head. 'No.'

'Neither had I.' Violet reached for her hand. 'Fayad's family took me to their heart and Bram's mother and sisters will do the same for you.'

Ruby swallowed and, realising that she was too full up to speak, Violet became brisk.

'The dress… There isn't much time. I've brought across some of my own collection but we'll measure you up, have a chat about what you like. Once we have an idea of your style Leila will have a selection of clothes sent up from the boutiques in the mall.'

Violet ushered her through to a less daunting room where comfortable sofas, piled with huge soft cushions, invited her to kick off her shoes and curl up. Rails of exotic clothes in glowing jewel colours had been lined up but, before she could look at them, Leila ran a tape measure over her and checked her shoe size. That done, the two of them flicked through the clothes, transferring those they thought would suit her to an empty rail.

Shot silks with Violet's trademark appliquéd designs, swirls of chiffon, deep reds to match her name, embroidered and beaded creations, each one costing more than she would earn in months.

'No…'

Violet turned. 'A bit over-the-top for your taste?'

'They are gorgeous,' she said, afraid that she'd offended the Princess. 'It's just that I usually wear black. Or grey. And I have a dress for this evening. It's designer,' she added a little desperately.

'Show me.'

'I don't know what's happened to my bag.'

'Noor is unpacking it for you,' Leila said.

Violet led the way through another, smaller, sitting room and then into a dressing room where a young woman had an ironing board set up, pressing each item as she unpacked it and then hung it in the cupboards that lined the room.

'This is Noor,' she said. 'You will need a companion, someone who knows her way around, to look after you. She speaks some English and she has family in Umm al Basr.'

She dropped a quick curtsey. 'Welcome, *sitti*.'

'Thank you, Noor,' Ruby said, trying not to show that she was totally overwhelmed.

Violet, meanwhile, had taken her little black dress from the wardrobe and was holding it up for a better look. 'This is it?'

'Yes. There's a bolero with long sleeves,' she

added, showing her the little jacket with its stand away collar. Then, feeling something more was required, 'It's my go-anywhere dress.'

'And absolutely perfect,' she said, as she flicked through the rest of her clothes. 'As you said, this is a working wardrobe but you have a distinctive style. Classic, a touch retro.' She smiled. 'A little bit Audrey Hepburn?'

'You've got me,' Ruby admitted. 'I do the books for a woman who owns a high-end worn-once boutique. In return she keeps her eye out for anything that she thinks will suit me.'

'She's done you proud,' she said with a smile, 'but, even though it's just a simple signing ceremony, we'll do everything we can to make it special.' She turned to Leila to show her the dress. 'What do you think?'

'Elegant, perfect for Bram's personal assistant, but His Highness Sheikh Ibrahim will expect his bride to be wearing something a little more decorative for the ceremony.' She thought for a moment. 'There's a dress in the new collection…'

Violet smiled. 'Two minds…' She turned to Noor and asked her to fetch it. 'And if you'll make those calls, Leila?' Leila nodded, leaving them alone. 'Let's go and have some tea while we're waiting.'

'I'm so sorry to put you to so much trouble.'

'It's no trouble,' she said, grinning broadly. 'I

think the whole thing is utterly romantic. I want to know everything. How long have you known one another? How did you meet…?'

Hours later, Ruby stood in front of a mirror in the vast luxurious bedroom. She had been bathed, had her hair, nails, make-up done by what felt like an army of maids and now she was wearing a whisper of the finest silver-grey silk and lace underwear that a billionaire Sheikh, in desperate need of a wife, could buy. But she'd seen neither hide nor hair of him since he'd driven away and left her to the tender ministrations of his cousin's wife.

She reminded herself that if she'd been his real intended bride he wouldn't have seen her for much longer than five hours, so it wasn't such a stretch.

'Ready?' Violet asked.

She took another look at her reflection, her legs stretched by the four-inch heels she was wearing—one of a hundred or more pairs that had arrived that afternoon. Four-inch heels and clever strips of the softest pale grey suede.

She'd had little say in the choice. Violet and Leila had gone through everything and chosen for her, leaving her with little to do but nod her approval because this kind of dressing was way above her pay grade.

'Ready,' she confirmed, her voice little more than a whisper.

A seamstress had stood by while Leila and Violet had nipped and tucked and now the dress slid over her body like a lover's sigh—a drift of silk and chiffon sparkling with thousands of crystals clustered thickly over the bodice, falling in sprays over her hips, glittering amongst the gathers as it fell to the floor.

Noor spent long minutes closing the tiny fastenings at the side until the dress fitted like a second skin. There were no sleeves but a cape of chiffon sparkled and flowed unlined from her shoulders to cover her arms in front and fall into a short train behind, a miracle of cut and design.

That done, all three stood back, waiting for her reaction.

It was simple, it was breathtaking and, just for a moment, Ruby wondered what it would be like to be Bram's Princess, not on paper, but for real…

'I don't know what to say.'

'That is always the effect we aim for,' Violet said before kissing her cheek, taking her hand and leading her out through a sitting room that was now stacked with boxes and bags filled with clothes, shoes, underwear, and into the vast reception room.

They stopped in the centre of the room. Leila adjusted the fall of the skirt. Violet arranged the train then stood back and took a photograph of her using her phone.

'Stunning,' she said. 'Absolutely stunning. I wish I could be here to see Bram's face…' Then, having kissed her again, they left her standing alone to await the arrival of her groom.

Her heart was racing and, in an attempt to slow it, reclaim control of her body if not her life, she closed her eyes. When she opened them again Bram was standing in front of her and her heart rate shot through the roof.

She had only seen in him in the most casual of clothes—a towel, a pair of shorts and a T-shirt, dusty riding clothes, the chinos he'd worn with a loose collarless shirt to travel into the city. Now he was wearing traditional robes.

Everything was simple, understated. A plain white *thaub* over which had been thrown the finest camel hair *bisht*, a fine white *keffiyeh* held in place by a plain black *egal* and at his waist he carried a traditional curved knife in a black and silver filigree scabbard. Simple, understated, regal, he was every inch the desert prince, but it was his facc that held her—his golden eyes, a jaw strong enough to slay dragons, the seductive curve of a lower lip that she wanted to suck into her mouth.

No, no, no—

'Wow…' she said, all faux brightness. 'Look at us.'

'Rabi…' his voice was unexpectedly soft '…you are every inch a princess.'

Rabi… She blinked. 'You do know that when we're married I'll expect you to remember my name.'

'Fayad thought an Arabic name would be more suitable for the contract. That it would please my father. Rabi was the nearest to your own. It means harvest.'

All afternoon Violet and Leila had talked about weddings. Their own, those of their friends. They'd shown her photographs of their children, assuming that she would soon be a mother, and she'd had to play along, smile as if she couldn't wait.

The name Bram had given her implied fertility, fecundity and the lie was like a cold hand squeezing her womb.

'Your father will like that,' she said as he put down the leather case he was carrying. He glanced up, frowning, clearly catching something in her tone. 'Good choice,' she added with the smile she'd once practised in the mirror. The smile she used to cover hurt, pain, the spiteful remarks of others. It had been so long since she'd used it that her cheeks creaked a bit, but it seemed to reassure him and, as he opened the case, she didn't have to pretend to catch her breath as he revealed the jewels within.

Her gasp was totally real.

'Oh, my…' she said, staring at the Art Deco parure of diamonds and rubies.

At one point, feeling that she had to add something to the dress, shoe, underwear debate, she'd suggested that perhaps she needed some colour to offset the silver-grey but Leila had it covered with ruby polish for her nails and colour for her mouth.

'You like it?' he asked.

'It's perfect… How did you know?'

He smiled. 'Violet sent me a photograph of the dress, although I have to say it looks a lot better on you than a tailor's dummy.'

She felt her cheeks warm as he continued to look at her and she said, 'You owe her, Bram. She must have had a thousand things to do today but she and Leila have overseen every detail.'

'I'll repay her when I donate to her charity tonight.' He turned to the case and picked up one of a pair of bracelets that nestled against the silk. 'Shall we begin?'

She raised her hand without a word and he fastened the wide cuff of diamonds and rubies over her left wrist. Was he taking care not to actually touch her or was that her imagination?

He repeated the performance with her right wrist and no, it was not her imagination. When the clasp proved awkward she saw that his hands were shaking, no doubt at the cost of this temporary arrangement, but the jewels, at least, could be returned when it was all over.

She held out her hands to look at the result.

Hers were shaking too, she realised, and he caught them and held them, held her gaze. If he thought that was going to steady her he couldn't have been more wrong.

'Are you going to be all right, Ruby?' he asked.

'Fine,' she managed through a throat that felt as if it had been stuffed with boulders. 'It's just that I've never worn anything quite so…sparkly.'

He laughed. 'Shall we try the collar?'

She nodded and he released her hands to pick up a necklace that was a simple V-shaped geometric collar of diamonds and rubies, with clusters of rubies forming hearts down the centre of the V.

It was set dressing, she told herself. Just set dressing. Like the dress, the shoes, the contract. All to convince his father that this was real.

'You seem taller,' he said as he lifted the collar to her throat.

'It's the shoes.' She lifted the skirt an inch to reveal a barely-there sandal, her ruby-painted toenails.

He glanced down and it seemed half a lifetime before he finally looked up. 'Very pretty,' he said, his face expressionless, 'but I'm going to have to ask you to bend forward a little.'

She dipped her head and as his fingers brushed against the back of her neck she struggled to control the shiver that rippled through her body, tightened her nipples into hard buds against the lace that he would see the moment she straightened.

After what seemed like an age with his arms around her, drowning in the scent of clean laundry, warm skin, something that might have been sandalwood, the clasp finally clicked into place. He stepped back and she could breathe again. Too soon…

The backs of his fingers brushed against her skin as he lifted the collar and eased it into place so that the row of hearts was perfectly vertical and the necklace echoed the neckline of the dress where it dipped between her breasts.

'How does that feel?' he asked.

'Heavy…' There was a heaviness in her breasts and low in her belly. An ache between her thighs. It had been a long time since she'd shared a bed with a man but with every touch the heat, the need, was building.

'It will soon be over,' he said, reaching for one of the earrings—long falls of diamonds and rubies.

'Shall I…?' she asked shakily. She was unravelling and if he touched her again…

'Your hands aren't steady enough.'

'Believe me, if you were wearing this many diamonds you'd be feeling a bit wobbly,' she said.

'You'll get used to it,' he assured her.

'Not in a million years and you wouldn't do

this for Bibi,' she said desperately, her knees, hips melting as women's bodies had melted since the morning Eve woke up and discovered Adam staring down at her.

'No, she would come ready gift-wrapped,' he agreed as he carefully fitted the earrings in place.

And it would be his duty to unwrap her. In her case he was doing the wrapping but it wasn't going to be Christmas for either of them.

'Are they comfortable?' he asked. 'Not too heavy?'

She shook her head and they brushed against her neck.

Finally he took the last item from the case, a curious piece of white gold, scattered with diamonds and rubies arranged in flower shapes.

'What is that?' she asked.

'Give me your left hand.'

She raised it and he took it in his, held it for a moment before sliding the confection onto her hand so that the gems sparkled along her thumb and index finger. 'A double ring,' he said, continuing to hold it.

'Did I say wow?' she asked.

'I think that's my line. No one is going to lift an eyebrow when I tell them that when you appeared at the fort yesterday morning I knew that I could never let you go. They'll only wonder why on earth it took me so long to figure it out.'

'A fabulous dress and a king's ransom in jewels will work wonders.'

'It takes more than that.' For a moment he just stood there looking at her, then seemed to catch himself. 'Ready?'

She nodded. 'I might need a hand in these heels.'

'Not a problem.'

He took her right hand, turned and tucked her arm beneath his and slowly, giving her time to become accustomed to the height of the heels, the length of the dress, the tug of the train, he led her across the courtyard to a limousine that was waiting to take them to the Emir's audience room.

Noor was waiting to arrange her dress and the train so that she could sit without crushing it, then she climbed into the front seat beside the driver so that she could make any final adjustments when they arrived.

Bram joined her, reached for her hand. It was all show from here on in…

He glanced at her. 'Are you still trembling?'

'It's just a touch of stage fright. I've never been married before.'

'That makes two of us,' he said with a smile that only made the butterflies worse. 'The trick is to remember that this is all make-believe.'

'Yes.' None of this was real so being nervous

was just plain silly and she was about to say so but the car came to a halt and the door was opened by whatever passed for a footman in this part of the world. It was like a scene from the evening news where one of the royals was arriving at a gala, even down to the red carpet.

Bram stepped out and turned to offer her a hand, tightening his grip as she steadied herself on the heels. He waited for a moment while Noor adjusted the folds of her skirt, her train, tweaked a curl into place and then loosely draped a scarf made from the same material as her dress, sparkling with crystals, over her hair.

Ruby stared up at the splendour of the floodlit dome at the centre of the palace complex as she took her time arranging the ends so that they trailed behind her to the floor.

'It looks like a picture in a book of fairy tales I had as a child,' she said. 'Scheherazade telling cliff-hanger stories so that she would live for one more day…' A shiver ran through her. 'Is your home like this?' she asked.

'Similar in layout. I have—had—a house there.'

'It's going to be very dusty after five years,' she said, making a feeble joke to cover her nerves. And then, as his eyes clouded, wished she hadn't. 'Don't worry; I'm familiar with the working end of a vacuum cleaner.'

He grinned. 'You Garland Girls are such good

value,' he said as he led her along the red carpet that had been laid not for them but in preparation for the arrival of guests for the banquet later that evening.

'Have you told your brother?' she asked as they entered a great central hall glittering with chandeliers. 'About this.'

'No.'

'You were afraid I'd change my mind?'

'It seemed wise to ensure that he was as shocked as everyone else.' He paused, turned to look down at her. 'You can still change your mind, Ruby. It's not too late.'

'I would never have let it go this far.'

'Even so.'

'We're keeping their Highnesses waiting,' she said and after a moment he moved on, leading her by the hand to a smaller, less intimidating room.

Ruby had imagined a host of people gathered to witness the occasion but there were only four people present: Princess Violet, Sheikh Fayad al Kuwani, Leila and another man who was presumably the Emir's aide.

On the table between them was an exquisitely modern floral arrangement—three perfect dark red roses progressing from a bud at the top to a fully open bloom at the bottom. There were three leather folders, presumably holding the marriage contracts—she wondered what they actually said—a gold pen and a seal. Two chairs had been placed facing the table.

She had been briefed by Leila and dropped a brief curtsey to the Emir and his Princess and, having received warm smiles from both of them, began to relax.

The formalities did not take long. First there were photographs, the two of them alone and then with the Emir and Princess Violet, taken by the aide.

Once they were all seated, he opened the leather folders, took more photographs of Bram signing the contracts and of his cousin signing on her behalf. He then applied the Emir's official seal to the documents and returned them to their folders.

Once that was done, Bram reached for her right hand, inviting her to stand before turning to his cousin. The Emir, smiling broadly, produced a ring, a circle of oval diamonds that blazed like fire in the light of the chandelier above them as he handed it to Bram.

A ring? That wasn't a tradition in this part of the world. A simple ceremony, the signing of a contract, was just business. A ring made it a wedding…

Bram held it for a moment between his thumb and forefinger and then, never taking his eyes from hers, spoke in Arabic as he placed the ring on the third finger of her right hand. Then, in

English, he said, 'Rabi al-Dance, you have honoured me by consenting to be my wife and I give you this ring as a sign that we are joined for ever.'

For ever...

She stared at it, then up at him, but before the question could form in her head Violet held out her hand and lying on her palm was a plain silver wedding band.

Bram's fingers tightened over hers and she saw that he had not anticipated this. However, there was nothing to be done but to take the ring and, having drawn in a steadying breath, place it on the third finger of his right hand. That done, she looked up.

'Ibrahim bin Tariq al-Ansari, you do me great honour by taking me as your wife,' she said. Then, repeating his pledge back to him, 'Wear this ring as a sign that we are joined for ever.'

And it was not a lie. They would be linked for ever by the secret they shared.

There was a moment of total silence and then there was a spontaneous burst of applause from their small audience before Violet, smiling from ear to ear, said, 'You have married an Englishwoman, Bram. Where we come from, it's traditional to kiss the bride.'

CHAPTER FIVE

BRAM FELT THE startled tremor ripple from Ruby's hand to his as Violet demanded a kiss for his bride but she lifted her face, not betraying by as much as a blink that this was an intimacy over and above what she'd signed up for.

Or maybe, once the rings had been produced, she had anticipated where this had been leading. The ceremony itself had been more than he'd bargained for when he'd asked his cousin to draw up the marriage contract but Fayad's English-born wife had been determined to make the moment special for her countrywoman and this was part of the show.

It was nothing. A formality. They were on a stage, acting out the story they had devised, and if the audience insisted on joining in it simply proved how successful they had been.

All that was required was the briefest touch of his lips but he instinctively lifted his hand to her face, cradling the soft curve of her cheek as he shielded her in this moment of intimacy. He felt the warmth of her breath as her mouth, red as the rubies he'd placed at her throat, parted on an intake of breath and sweet, soft lips trembled against his.

Or maybe it was him because he couldn't have been more wrong about this kiss.

This was that moment when he'd looked up and seen her silhouette against the lowering sun, the moment when she'd stumbled on the steps and he'd held her close, felt her curves fit him as if they were one and knew the scent of her hair, her skin. In that moment the heat of possession surged through him and he became the groom he was supposed to be—primed to fight his way through the throng of her family, overcome his bride's reluctance to surrender her honour and claim her as his own and his kiss became a brand.

The flash as someone took a photograph, a smattering of applause, brought him to his senses. As he raised his head Ruby opened eyes that were more black than grey; her cheeks were flushed, her bee-stung lips slightly parted as if on a breath that was stuck in her throat.

'The official photographs are for your father,' Violet said, apparently noticing nothing amiss in the reaction of two people who had supposedly been lovers for more than a year and had now chosen to make a lifelong commitment. This was a life-changing moment: stunned was the perfect response. 'For the family album. I'll have copies printed to put with the contracts but this one,' she said, grinning as she thumbed something into her phone, 'is just for you.'

And then Fayad was hugging him, shaking his hand, and Violet and Leila were kissing Ruby.

'I'm so sorry that we cannot raise a toast to you both at dinner this evening,' Violet said, 'but Fayad has explained that Bram wishes to keep the news under wraps until he has told his father.'

'We'll celebrate properly when you return,' Fayad said as they walked back through the vast audience chamber and out into a courtyard that was now lit with thousands of white fairy lights in preparation for the evening. 'Or will you be staying in Umm al Basr?'

'If all goes well I hope to spend time there but the fort is my home,' he said. Behind him, Violet—walking with Ruby—gave a little cough, reminding him of his changed status and, feeling exactly like the awkward, new-to-this groom he was supposed to be, he looked back. 'Our home.' And he reached back for Ruby's hand, enfolding it in his as he gave it a squeeze of reassurance. 'Give me a minute, *ya habibati*, this is all very new.'

'Yes.' The word came on a little gasp that exactly echoed the way he was feeling and he wanted to tell her that she'd been amazing, tell her…

Tell her nothing.

This was a business arrangement. Six months' salary. Plus the fee to pay her lawyer. And the financial settlement due to the wife of the Sheikh in the event of divorce that Fayad had negotiated on her behalf. They had been writing prenuptial agreements in this part of the world long before the Californians thought of them.

'I'm sorry for rushing you away, but I have to check the last-minute details for tonight's banquet.' Violet's apology as they reached their car was no more than a formality—from her very un-princess-like grin it was clear she believed they couldn't wait to get back to their apartment.

Instead they were sitting an arm's width apart in the rear of the limousine taking them back to their apartment with that kiss sizzling between them. They might be playing newlyweds on a strictly business basis, but all he could think about was the silk of her cheek beneath his hand. The heated welcome of her mouth. What it would be like if this were real…

Ruby cleared her throat. '*Ya hab…?*' She struggled for the word.

'*Ya habibati*,' he said, keeping his eyes straight ahead. 'A woman would say *ya habibi*.'

'Only if she knew what it meant. It's not a word I've come across in my *Arabic for Beginners*.'

'Beloved.' He turned and looked at her. 'It means *my beloved*.'

'Oh.' The diamonds he'd placed at her throat sparkled as she swallowed.

'We tend to be extravagant in our endearments.'

Making a determined effort to get them back on a businesslike footing, but keeping her eyes on the back of the driver's head, she said, 'Perhaps you should teach me some…' She faltered. 'I should know them.'

'We are not in the west,' he replied, hanging onto his self-control by a thread. 'Here, intimacy is a private thing.'

He had been sharp and she did not reply. Maybe she understood—she seemed to have a rare, instinctive understanding of most things—that he'd been caught without a defence against a kiss that he hadn't anticipated, for which he had not been prepared.

He'd had more freedom than his brother—he'd been indulged, given time to enjoy the sports he'd loved, because there would come a time when he'd have to assume the mantle of responsibility, put his people before his own pleasures—but he'd always known that marriage was a rare and precious thing, an alliance of honour between a man and woman whose future had been written for the benefit of family and state.

Right now he was in the grip of a physical response to an age-old need but this was not a flirtation with a chalet maid or one of the snow bunnies who followed the sport. This was… This was strictly business.

After what seemed a lifetime of silence the car

stopped, the door opened and he was able to step out, draw in a lungful of the cool evening air before turning to offer Ruby his hand.

He sensed her reluctance to take it; he wasn't the only one who'd been swept away by that kiss. Hampered by the dress and the height of her heels, however, she had no choice but to lay her hand against his as she stepped from the car. Aware that they were still on show, that unseen eyes would follow their every move, he continued to hold her hand as he escorted her into their apartment.

Once there, she couldn't wait to let go of his hand as she kicked off her shoes and headed for the bedroom with an abrupt, 'I have to get out of this dress.'

Bram had kissed her. Neither of them had anticipated it. The ceremony was supposed to be a formal signing of the contracts, but clearly Violet had other ideas. The dress, the jewels, the perfectly fitting rings…

He had placed a circle of diamonds on her finger, made a public vow with a private meaning and then he'd kissed her. It should have been little more than a formal touch of his lips but she could still feel his hand against her cheek, the heat of his mouth…

She needed a moment, time on her own to put

the pieces back together but, as she reached the bedroom door, she stopped in her tracks.

While they'd been plighting their troth, Noor had dressed it for the arrival of the bride and groom.

There were roses. Dark red roses that filled the air with a heavy scent.

On the long, low table that stood at the foot of the bed a silver bowl had been filled with sugar-frosted fruit. Beside it was a tray of sweets—Turkish Delight, truffles, tiny pastries and nuts. A silver-lidded glass jug filled with some dark red juice, another of water, stood in a casket of ice. Everything to refresh them, sustain them, as they consummated their marriage.

And the white damask spread that covered the bed had been scattered with ruby-red rose petals…

Her mouth opened but nothing emerged.

Noor, waiting to help her out of the dress, take it back to Violet's workshop, dropped a shy little curtsey and said, 'Congratulations, *sitti, sidi*.'

Sitti…

'It means Lady.' Bram, at her shoulder, eased her into the room.'

'Yes…I know…' She'd heard Violet addressed that way by the staff bringing deliveries from the boutiques in the mall. '*Shukran*, Noor.'

Bram dismissed the girl with a word as he unfastened his belt and tossed the *khanjar* he was wearing onto a sofa. A sweep of his hand and his *keffiyeh* followed it and the girl ducked her head, giggling, as she scurried to the door.

He kicked it shut behind her.

'Bram!' she protested.

'She will tell Leila that I was impatient,' he said. 'Leila will tell Violet and tonight Fayad will give her a son, a cousin to grow up as a companion for our firstborn.'

The image was so vivid that her legs buckled and her protest was no more than a small noise at the back of her throat and, without warning, his arm was around her, steadying her. 'And so the legend grows,' he said with a wry twist of his mouth.

'Well, that's great,' she said, horribly conscious of the blush heating her cheeks, his body keeping her upright, his mouth just inches from her own. 'Unfortunately, it leaves me in a dress that I can't get out of without help.'

'An impatient groom would tear it off you. Maybe, in the pursuit of reality…?'

'Don't even think it, Bram Ansari!' she said, finding the strength to pull away. 'Violet loaned me this dress to please you. It's to be the centrepiece of her new collection and it took weeks to make.'

'Then it's a good thing that I can handle a zip.'

He turned to the table, poured juice into a glass, glanced at her but she shook her head.

'I don't doubt your familiarity with the zip fastening,' she snapped. She'd seen that photograph in the fountain. Which was none of her business, she told herself. 'Unfortunately, this isn't a dress I picked up in a high street boutique. It is handmade couture, made to look as if it was created on my body.'

His sipped the glowing red juice, his gaze an almost physical touch as it lingered on the way it clung to her breasts, her waist, how it flared at the hips.

'There are tiny hidden hooks and eyes,' she said, before he said something outrageous. 'Little stitches where Noor fitted it to me.'

'We have an hour to kill. Hunting for invisible fastenings will pass the time.' He replaced the glass on the tray, his eyes dark, his lids hooded and she shivered, not with fear but anticipation. Her head might have signed up for the no-sex deal but her body appeared to be on another planet. 'If you'll give me a clue where to start?'

'Don't worry about it. I'll manage somehow,' she said, unhooking the earrings and laying them carefully on the table beside the tray of sweets. The bracelets caused her more trouble and he made a move to help but she fended him off with a look that must have summed up all the frustration she was feeling because he raised his hands in a gesture of surrender, took a step back. She should be happy about that but she was not supposed to be feeling anything. Certainly not disappointment.

The ruby and diamond cuff on her left wrist slipped off after a bit of a tussle with the safety catch. The one on her right wrist defeated her and she let out a little puff of frustration.

'I'm sorry,' he said, but he didn't look it. He looked as if he was struggling not to laugh.

'It's not funny, Bram.'

'No.' He straightened his face. 'You were right, *sitti*. I should not have sent away your maid.'

'Then call her back.'

'And have the entire palace know that my bride cared more about a dress than satisfying her husband?'

'Damn it, Bram!' She shook her head. 'I'm sorry. It's just that I've spent most of the day being carried along on the current of Violet's excitement. I was going to wear my black dress but no one was listening to me.'

'I'm sorry.' They looked at one another and then, because it was so ridiculous, they both laughed.

'Shall we stop apologising to one another, Bram? We knew this wasn't going to be easy.'

'When I spoke to Fayad last night it never occurred to me that there would be any kind of ceremony but Violet wanted to make the day memorable for you.'

'She succeeded beyond her wildest dreams but I should been have been firmer. At least about the dress.'

'Remember that when you meet my sisters,' he said. 'Given free rein with my credit cards, they will be unstoppable.'

'I don't need any more clothes,' she said.

'Don't tell them that. They'll think you're crazy.'

'I think I'm crazy,' she replied.

'Undoubtedly, but in the meantime if you don't let me help you we are never going to make the banquet this evening.'

'Do we have to go?' she asked. 'The thought of an entire evening pretending one thing to Violet and Fayad—' she wouldn't have the least trouble blushing '—and something else to everyone else…' She swallowed. It shouldn't be a problem. She'd spent all her adult life pretending… 'Do *I* have to go?' she added quickly.

He smiled, shaking his head. 'Ruby, Ruby, Ruby…'

'Forget I said that,' she said, realising just too late how that would look. She held out her wrist. 'Just concentrate on the bracelet.'

He took her hand but seemed to find it no easier than when he'd fastened it. 'The safety catch on this one is tougher to crack than Fort Knox.'

'You wouldn't want anything flimsy on something so valuable,' she said, doing her best to ignore the cool touch of his fingers, the delicious slide of his dark hair over his forehead as he bent over her wrist, the waft of pheromones that had her hormones whizzing around in a frenzy.

She had met many attractive men as she'd moved from company to company and there had been invitations to carry the day over into the evening but she'd never once been tempted to mix business with pleasure. She knew, as they did not, that there would have been no future in it.

There was a big difference between the boardroom and the bedroom, however. The arrangement with Bram involved the kind of intimacy that she'd never encountered in the office. The only way she could see this through was by being totally professional. And taking a cold shower the minute she was out of this dress.

The cuff finally parted and he tossed the bracelet beside its pair as if it was no more than a trinket from the market.

'The necklace?' he prompted.

She half turned so that he could reach the fastening. 'Don't step on the train!' she warned.

He scooped it up and dumped it in her arms. 'Just keep still while I try and figure this out. I've had more practice putting jewels on a woman than taking them off and they're a lot trickier than a zip.'

A little dart of something sharp, something green, shot through her at the thought of him dressing other women in precious stones and her hands tightened into little fists all by themselves. Realising that she was creasing the material, she forced herself to relax. It was ridiculous to feel jealous of the women who'd passed through his life.

She was the one wearing the diamond and ruby collar that was causing him so much trouble. It was her neck his fingers were touching, sending a charge as if she'd touched a live wire rippling through her.

She was the one he'd turned to, trusted not to betray him.

'Ruby,' he protested as she twitched nervously.

About to apologise, she caught her lip and lowered her head to his shoulder to make it easier for him to gain access to the clasp, her face in the snowy white of his robes, breathing in the scent of fresh linen, soap, warm skin. It would be so easy to let the train fall, reach for him, hold him…

He muttered something as the clasp finally parted and he stepped back. 'I think I broke it.'

'The jeweller will repair it when you return it,'

she said, taking it from him, laying it carefully beside the cuffs.

He looked as if he was going to say something but when she waited he shook his head. 'Can you manage the rest?'

'Of course,' she said, sliding off the double ring he'd placed on her hand with little regret. It was pretty, but would catch on her clothes, her stockings. 'I know how Cinderella felt when the clock struck twelve,' she said, making a joke of it as she slipped off the diamond wedding band.

'Your clock has months to run before midnight strikes but your coach won't turn into a pumpkin. You will keep the ring and the title that goes with it.'

She looked up, startled. 'I can't do that,' she protested.

'Complain to Fayad. It's in the contract he negotiated on your behalf.'

'And you agreed?' Stupid. Of course he did. He was supposed to be in love. 'I won't use it. And I can't keep the ring either.'

'You are giving me back my family, Ruby. Six months of your life. That is worth a lot more than a few diamonds.'

'Six months?' They hadn't got around to discussing how long they would have to keep up the pretence. 'You want me to stay until September?'

'Even the most hasty and ill-conceived marriage needs time to fall apart.'

'You think? I've seen celebrity marriages that have lasted less than six days.'

He shrugged. 'No doubt, but I'd like to put off the break-up until I'm sure that Bibi is safely settled in Cambridge.'

'You're suggesting that if it's too soon there might be pressure to revert to Plan A?'

'That's one reason,' he agreed, with one of those rare smiles that seemed to light her up from the inside.

'And the other?' she asked, her voice not quite steady.

'It will take time to replace Peter.'

'Oh. Yes…' What on earth had she expected him to say? Six days, six months—it was just a job. She'd made a commitment and once she was wearing her own sensible clothes, away from the heady scent of roses, the sparkle of diamonds, the need to pretend, she would be fine.

'Will you call Jude Radcliffe and break the news?' she asked, cranking up a smile to let him know that she was okay with his plan, 'or will I?'

'Leave it to me,' he said, the creases in his face deepening into a smile. 'It's the least I can do, under the circumstances.'

She nodded, her smile fading as she looked down at the circle of diamonds lying in the palm of her hand. 'This is the most beautiful ring I've ever seen but I'll forever be worrying about losing it in a washroom. An old-fashioned plain gold wedding band that you never take off is a lot more practical.'

'A princess does not have to think of practicalities.'

She rolled her eyes and got another smile for her effort.

'On the subject of practicalities,' she said. 'As your personal assistant, I'd advise you to remove your own ring before you forget.'

'Do you think anyone would notice it?' he asked, looking at the plain silver band she'd placed on his finger.

She arched a brow at him. 'Hello… Single, sexy billionaire, undoubtedly the most eligible man in the room? Allegedly.'

'Most of the women there will be with husbands or partners,' he reminded her.

'You think that will deter them? You must have been leading a more sheltered life than you'd have me believe.'

'Are you suggesting that I'll be propositioned?'

'Isn't that why you need your PA with you?' she asked. 'To ensure there's an orderly queue. That is if I ever get out of this dress. It will do your image no good if Noor returns to help me dress for this evening and I'm still wearing it,' she pointed out and, certain that she had everything under control, she lifted her arm so that he could reach the tiny hooks holding the dress together.

She was wrong.

It started well enough but the combination of the cool air and the touch of his fingers skimming her skin as the dress slowly parted from breast to hip sent a shiver rippling through her and she grabbed his shoulder for support.

'It's done,' he said at last.

'Thank you.' She was forced to clear her throat. 'If you'll just help me get it over my head.'

'*Tawaqqal!* Enough.' He took a step back and her hand slid from his shoulder. 'The dress is yours. No one else will wear it.'

She clamped her lips shut against a protest. If she was trembling from the intimacy of the moment, how much worse must it be for Bram?

'I'm sorry,' he said. 'I did not mean to shout at you.'

'Don't…I wasn't thinking…' She drew in a slow breath, gathered herself. 'For me this is just a job. For you…'

For him it was a chance to return home, but at what cost?

He was a man who'd been born to lead and he'd done that all his life. On the ski slopes, on horseback, in the financial market. Now, when he could have had it all—a good political marriage that would restore him to the succession—he'd turned his back on the prize because… Because the girl chosen as his bride wanted to be a doctor?

Really?

How likely was that?

She didn't doubt Bibi Khadri's ambitions; she'd had ambitions of her own but there was a world of difference between a dream and reality. And what girl would rather be a doctor than the wife of the Emir? To be Umm al Basr's first lady? With jewels, clothes—everything she desired.

Had she really begged her sister for help or had Bram's brother, aware that the crown was slipping from his grasp, invented the smuggled note to keep him away? And, if so, why on earth did he imagine that Bram would care?

She took a step back. 'I'll manage,' she said quickly, picking up her skirt and heading for the privacy of the dressing room so that she could think.

Bram stared for a moment at the closed door. He should never have allowed that to happen. He'd made Ruby a promise and he should have been able to help her out of a dress without making a fool of himself, but sending that girl away—as if he had been a real groom and Ruby had been his bride—had been an instinctive reaction. Not exactly fighting his way through her male relations to claim her, but it was right out of that tradition and he retreated to his own dressing room, shed his robes and took a cold shower.

Ruby wriggled carefully out of the dress and placed it on a padded hanger. If Noor was disappointed that he hadn't torn it off her in a fit of passion… Well, it wasn't as if she was his new bride, seen for the first time, claimed…

She stopped the thought, stripped off and stepped under a cool shower.

Five minutes later, having forcefully reminded herself why she was here, she wrapped herself in a soft towelling robe, opened her tablet and logged into Bram's email account, made a note of who needed to be responded to as a matter of urgency. Then, having restored herself to PA mode, she began to get ready for the charity dinner.

Noor had laid out her dress for the evening, along with a set of filmy black lace underwear. Realising that it would look odd if she discarded it in favour of her own rather more functional underclothes, she slipped them on and then covered them with her black dress and the matching long-sleeved bolero that covered her arms.

There was a new pair of delicious black suede peep-toe shoes parked neatly side by side that Noor had chosen for her to wear. They were utterly gorgeous and she could not resist slipping her feet into them, checking them out in the mirror. She was seriously tempted to keep them on but the heels were ridiculously high and a hard-working PA needed to be quick on her feet and, reluctantly, she changed into her own black ballet flats. Finally she fastened the single strand of pearls and matching pearl ear studs that her mother had been given on her eighteenth birthday, slipped on the ruby ring that had been in her family for over a hundred years and checked her reflection.

It was reassuringly familiar. She was Ruby Dance, in-demand temporary personal assistant, and she had a job to do. Speaking of which…

She straightened her back, opened the door to the bedroom and, relieved to see that it was empty—she really did not want a witness for this—wasted no time in messing up the bed.

Rose petals scattered across the floor as she pulled back the cover, tugged loose the sheet, punched the pillows to look as if they had been used, knocking one onto the floor in the process.

Heart pounding, she stepped back to check the effect. It would do, she decided, and turned her back on the mess, only to discover that Bram, immaculate in a dinner jacket, was watching her from the doorway of his own dressing room on the far side of the room.

'I just…' She made an attempt at a shrug, aware that she was blushing. Which was ridiculous.

'I saw.' He crossed to the table at the foot of the bed, poured some water into a glass, taking a sip as he walked around the bed examining her handy work.

Work. Concentrate on that. She cleared her throat. 'You've had a couple of urgent…'

Her voice trailed away as he stretched his arm out over the bed and tilted the glass, spilling a little of the water onto the centre of the rumpled sheet.

A completely involuntary sound escaped her lips and he said, 'For future reference, Ruby, if you're going to fake a scene you have to pay attention to the details.' When she didn't answer he glanced back. 'A couple of urgent what?'

'Emails…' Her mouth made all the right moves but no sound emerged and she cleared her throat again. 'Emails. One from Michael Shadbrook about setting up a meeting on Friday in London. One from Jimmy Rose in Hong Kong. He's been trying to call you.'

'I've spoken to him,' he said, his tone brisk and businesslike, as if he hadn't just left a damp patch on the bed… 'We can fly on to London from Dubai on Thursday morning. I'll leave you to organise a time, sort out the details and let Shadbrook know. Is there anything else?'

Clearly her boring little black dress was doing the job.

'Will you want to return here to Ras al Kawi or Umm al Basr before going to Mumbai?' she asked.

'Let's see how it goes tomorrow,' he said briskly. 'Is that it?'

'Yes. Have I got time to do it now?'

He glanced at his wristwatch. 'You have fifteen minutes.'

She retreated to the sitting room, sat at a small desk and, keeping an eye on the time, swiftly organised the flight, warned the Savoy that he would be in residence at his service flat on Thursday and possibly Friday night—she would stay in her own flat—changed his booking in Dubai for a suite with two bedrooms and emailed Michael Shadbrook to let him know that Bram Ansari would be available to meet him at eleven o'clock on Friday morning.

She finished with a minute spare and she used that to go and change into those pretty suede shoes that Noor had left out for her.

The dinner was over. Bram, waiting while Ruby received a farewell hug from Violet, paused to have a word with Nigel and Lorraine Grieg, the British Ambassador and his wife, who were waiting for their car.

He turned as she re-joined him but, before he could introduce her, Lorraine said, 'Jools? Jools

Howard, Future World Champion?' She laughed. 'What on earth are you doing here?'

Jools?

Ruby who, despite her earlier reservations, had sailed through the evening completely at ease in whatever company she found herself, lost every scrap of colour from her face.

She'd told him that she'd changed her name after some scandal but not just her family name, it seemed. Ruby was not her real first name…

'My wife answers to Princess Rabi these days,' he said when the silence went on for too long.

'Princess…?' Lorraine Grieg looked from Ruby to him and back again but this time it was Nigel who leapt diplomatically into the breach.

'Congratulations, Bram,' he said, offering his hand. 'I had no idea you'd finally given up the bachelor life.'

'It's a recent development,' he said. 'There has been no public announcement.'

Nigel met his eye. He knew the situation with his father and instantly got the message. 'I understand,' he said, and turned to Ruby. 'My best wishes, Princess Rabi.'

'Thank you.' Given a moment's breathing space, Ruby had swiftly recovered her poise if not her colour, painted on a smile. 'I'm sorry, Lori—' She went through the air kiss ritual and anyone who didn't know Ruby would have thought she was delighted at having found an old friend. It was an impressive performance but he'd seen her smile when she meant it and realised that he'd seen this smile too. It wouldn't fool him again. 'Seeing you was so unexpected. It quite took my breath away. How long has it been?'

'Not since school…' Lorraine faltered, clearly remembering something unpleasant, and turned to her husband. 'You should have seen her on horseback, darling. Such a star. We were all convinced that she would come away from the London Olympics with a handful of gold medals. Do you still ride?'

'No.' Ruby's smile slipped and, without thinking, he reached for her hand.

'These days she's my star.'

'So sweet.' Lorraine smiled indulgently. 'Perhaps we could get together for lunch soon, Jools? Catch up on all the news?'

He didn't need the tremor in her hand to know how little she relished the prospect and he tightened his grip. 'We'll be away for a week or two, but why don't you both come out to Qa'lat al Mina'a when we return?' he suggested as their car, flying the Union flag, pulled up alongside them. 'I'll give you a call, Nigel.'

They waited while they boarded, returning a wave as they were borne away down the hill and out of sight.

'Bram—'

'Not here,' he said, tucking her arm under his so that she could lean on him as they headed away from the central dome of the palace and through the palace gardens.

'Bram, I'm so sorry. I n-never imagined…' She had hung onto her composure but now reaction was setting in. Her teeth were chattering and she was struggling to catch her breath. 'I c-c-can't…'

She buckled against him and, with a muttered curse, he caught her and, arm about her waist, supported her to a seat set in the privacy of a jasmine-covered arbour. She was shivering, more with shock than cold, but he took off his jacket, slipped it around her shoulders and then put his arm around her and held her close.

CHAPTER SIX

BRAM'S JACKET WAS warm from his body, his arm was around her and Ruby's cheek was pressed against fresh linen, the steady beat of his heart. This was the hug she'd been dreaming about, yearning for ever since her world fell apart and for a moment she soaked it up, knowing that, like so much of these few days, it would be a treasured memory. But he hadn't signed up for this. He wanted an uncomplicated, no-strings temporary wife not a baggage-laden emotional wreck.

'Th-thank you,' she said, summoning every scrap of inner strength to ease away, sit up. 'Thank you for rescuing me back there.'

'I thought you were going to faint,' he said, his hand still at her back.

'I thought I was,' she admitted. 'But I meant when Lori said my name.'

'So did I, but it was a great recovery. She had no idea.'

'You knew,' she said.

'Our relationship has been short but intense,' he said, 'and I wasn't distracted with the problem of who I was going to text the minute the car arrived.'

'No.' She managed some sort of smile. 'You read her pretty well too.'

'I've met her before.' He glanced at her. 'Jools?'

'It's what I was called at school. It's short for Juliet.'

She risked a glance in his direction. His profile was lit by the soft lighting hidden amongst the branches and she couldn't read his expression but it wasn't that which was making her shiver. It was being forced to confront memories that she'd buried deep, locked away. Memories that she'd been hiding from for years. 'I'm sorry, Bram.'

'I thought we'd banned the word *sorry*?'

'But I should have told you before all this…' She made a gesture that took in the palace, the gardens, everything that had happened that day.

'Tell me now,' he said.

'Yes…' And, doing her best to ignore the cold, sick feeling in the pit of her stomach, she said, 'I was born Juliet Dorothea Howard.' There was no response but there was no reason for him to remember a sordid story that had filled the headlines ten years ago. 'My home was a small manor house that had been in my mother's family for ever and, until I was sixteen, I had the kind of life that most people dream about.'

She let her eyes flicker in his direction. His arm was still a comforting support but, although he'd turned to look down at her, his face remained impassive, giving no clue as to what he might be thinking.

'A week after my sixteenth birthday my father was exposed as a con man who preyed on vulnerable, older women. He wooed them, seduced them and when they were putty in his hands, ready to sign anything he put in front of them, he robbed them.'

She opened the elegant little shoulder bag that contained her phone, tapped her father's name into the search engine, clicked on a link and handed it to him.

'It's all there.'

She fixed her eyes on the glowing dome of the palace as he skimmed through the newspaper story that had brought her world crashing down.

After a few minutes he handed the phone back to her. 'You were sixteen years old, Ruby. None of this has anything to do with you.'

'Tell that to the photographers who camped outside my school gates, the reporters who rang my mobile phone day and night, wanting a comment, an interview, anything… According to them, I was a pampered princess living a lifestyle that most people could only dream about.'

'They hounded you?' He didn't sound surprised.

'Of course they hounded me. I didn't rob those poor women of their savings, their pension funds, their self-worth, Bram, but my little ponies were the real thing and I was having the most expensive, most privileged education that the money my father stole from them could buy.'

'But the school protected you?'

'They kept the gates locked, refused to comment, but they couldn't stop the long-range lenses, keep out the photographers who climbed the walls,' she said, wrapping her arms about herself as if she could hold in the pain. 'Stop the girls who used their phones to send in photographs that they'd snapped during the year, of me fooling around in the pool, giggling at impromptu birthday parties, on prize-giving day with my father. I was desperate to go home, to be with my mother, but the house, the village, was besieged by the media and the head smuggled me out of school and I was in Scotland before anyone realised I'd gone.'

'Scotland?'

'My mother's old nanny had retired there.'

'You had no other family to turn to?'

She shook her head. 'My grandmother died very young and my mother stayed at home to care for her increasingly frail father. When he died she inherited a house that had been in her family for centuries, what was left of the original estate, a couple of cottages and a London flat. She was in her mid-thirties and alone in the world, apart from a few distant ageing cousins she had only met at funerals.'

'The perfect mark for a man who preyed on vulnerable women.'

'The death notices, obituaries, the publication of wills are meat and drink to a con man.' Restless, unable to sit there a moment longer, she said, 'Can we walk?'

He stood up and, his arm still around her, they walked back through the gardens towards their apartment. The palace was built on the highest point of the city and far out in the Gulf she could see the lights of a ship heading out towards the Indian Ocean.

'It's so peaceful here,' she said, pausing to watch its stately progress. 'You could hear a star fall.'

'They don't make much of a splash.'

She glanced at him. Was that humour? Sarcasm? There was nothing in his voice to give her a clue and his face was all shadows.

'Your mother was the perfect mark but, instead of robbing her, he married her,' he prompted after a while. 'Did he fall in love with her?'

'Making people believe he loved them was just something he did to get what he wanted, Bram.'

'So?'

'He fell in love with the image.' His lack of emotion made it easier. 'He saw a lovely old manor house with a couple of cottages and a hundred acres of grazing land bringing in a tidy income. There were ancient wax jackets hanging in the mud room, good-looking Labradors in front of a log fire and a perfect chocolate box Cotswold village. He didn't steal my mother's inheritance, Bram; he moved into it. He became part of the community, always ready with a generous donation for repairs to the church hall or the cricket club pavilion. Always good company in the pub with his fund of stories about adventures hunting down new oil fields for his clients.'

'That was his cover for his absences?'

She nodded. 'He used to bring me little souvenirs. A perfect desert rose, a fossil, an amethyst geode from somewhere in Africa. A little meteorite that he'd picked up in the Arctic.'

Precious, precious things that she had cherished, clung to through his long absences. All bought from specialist shops. All lies.

'Did you ever doubt that he loved you?'

'No.' The word stuck in her throat. 'No, I never doubted that he loved me but I was just part of his picture-perfect family. His English rose wife whose family tree made the upstart Tudors look like newcomers. His little girl on her pony at the local gymkhana. It was a fairy tale with him as the handsome stranger who'd arrived out of nowhere to woo the lonely princess.'

'But without the happily ever after.'

'No.' She fought down the lump in her throat, wanting this over. 'I was taking part in the show-jumping at the county show and the friend of a woman he'd relieved of her savings spotted him with me in the collecting ring. His hair was a different colour, he'd shaved off the beard he'd grown for the con but she saw him smile up at me...'

She faltered. He would remember what she'd said about Oliver Brent, know where the expression had come from, and she felt naked, exposed...

'What did she do, Ruby?'

'She went to the local police, certain he was running one of his scams. They assured her that she was mistaken. Mr Howard was a well-known and respected member of the community.' She rushed on, wanting this over. 'Realising that she wasn't going to get anywhere with the police, she took her story to one of the tabloids. They ran the standard background checks and discovered that no one in the oil industry had heard of Jack Howard and there was no trace of him before he met my mother.'

'If he'd had any idea it was going to be a permanent identity he'd have taken more care but I imagine after so many years he thought he was safe. Did they ever discover his real name?'

She shook her head. She had no idea who her father really was. He had denied everything and, despite all the publicity, no one had ever come forward to claim him as a son, brother, father...

'They watched, waited and when he moved in on a new mark they told her what he was up to and asked her to play along. They installed hidden cameras, recorded all his phone calls and when they had it all they ran a big exposure piece before handing everything over to the police.'

'They wanted their story before reporting restrictions were imposed.'

'They wanted other victims to come forward. Some did but who knows how many were too embarrassed to admit to their family, friends what had happened to them?'

'You said they were both dead, Ruby?'

She looked up at him. 'You think I lied about that? That he's in jail?' She didn't wait for him to answer. 'My father was sent to the Crown Court for trial but cases like that take an age to prepare and he had a good lawyer. He was granted bail on the condition that he surrendered his passport, stayed at his home address and reported regularly to the local police station. When he missed his appointment they went to the house and discovered them both. The autopsy found horse tranquilliser.'

'A suicide pact?'

'That was the coroner's verdict but my father was a sociopath, Bram. He had no conscience.' Holding onto her emotions by a thread, she said, 'It was my mother who was suffering. She'd been cut dead by friends, neighbours, people she'd known all her life.'

'He had fooled them all. They would have been angry, embarrassed.'

'Yes…' The word caught in her throat.

'I was wrong when I said he hadn't stolen from her. He stole her life and now he's stealing yours.' He muttered something under his breath. 'That's why you asked about publicity. You didn't want to risk being recognised.'

She shrugged. 'At least you have the perfect excuse to divorce me.'

'I wouldn't use this.'

He looked almost angry at the suggestion. 'No one would blame you,' she said, 'but it's all academic now. Lori will already be texting gossipy messages to her old school chums and the story is too good not to pass on. Sooner or later it will leak.' He wouldn't use the story, but he wouldn't have to. It had all worked out perfectly.

She eased away from his arm, pulled his jacket around her. 'Thank you, Bram.'

'For what?'

For not judging her. For understanding. 'For listening.' She hunched her shoulders. 'That's all. Just listening.'

'You thought I would be angry?'

'You have every right. I told you I'd changed

my name because of a family scandal and you accepted that.'

'If I'd known the whole story,' he said, 'I would have still gone ahead.'

She nodded. Of course he would. He'd wanted an unsuitable wife and he'd got one with capital letters.

'Come,' he said. 'You've had a shock. What you need is a cup of tea.'

'Tea?' Despite everything, she laughed. 'How long did you live in England, Bram?'

'Too long, apparently,' he said as, with a wry smile, he put his arm around her, encouraging her to lean against him.

'No,' she said, her head against his shoulder. 'Just long enough.'

They walked back to the apartment where Noor, working on an exquisite piece of embroidery, was waiting to help her undress.

'There's no need to stay, Noor. I can manage.'

Bram added something in Arabic and she bobbed a curtsey, said goodnight and left.

Ruby slipped off his jacket, placed it over the back of a chair while he crossed to a table where a kettle and a tray of tea things had been left.

'Let me do that,' she protested.

'Sit,' he said, filling the kettle from a bottle of water and switching it on. 'Tell me what happened to you.' He turned and glanced at her. 'Afterwards.'

'Nothing. I stayed with my mother's nanny in Scotland while the lawyers dealt with the fall-out.' She shrugged. 'She was getting frail, needed looking after more than I did, so I signed up for a business course at a local college, using her name.'

'And your home?'

'Sold. I could never go back there.'

'No… And I imagine the victims' lawyers lined up with compensation claims.'

'There wasn't as much as they'd hoped. The house and its contents, the cottages, the family jewellery, the London flat had all been inherited by my mother and on her death passed to me. Since I was a minor, the proceeds from the sale of the house and the rest of her estate went into a trust until I was twenty-one.'

'As was right.'

'My father hadn't been tried, found guilty, but lawyers representing my interests agreed that his estate should be liquidised and the funds split between anyone who could prove that he'd stolen from them. His bank accounts, his cars, personal possessions.' She lifted her hand to her chest to relieve what was still a physical pain. 'The horses he'd bought for me.'

'Your horses? That's why you stopped riding?'

'I'm sure the lawyers would have released money to keep me riding, Bram, but can you imagine sitting up there, taking part in competitions with everyone looking at me, knowing what had happened? Can you imagine what the newspapers would have done with that?'

'I have a very good idea.' His face was expressionless but she knew he was remembering what had happened to him.

'I just wanted to disappear.'

'Yes…' For a moment their eyes met. After his disgrace he'd disappeared from the ski circuit, stopped playing polo, vanished from the society pages. 'In my case the damage was self-inflicted.'

'Why?' The question slipped out before she could stop it.

He frowned. 'Why?'

'It was out of character.' He raised an eyebrow. 'You appeared in the society magazines, lined up with other aristocrats and dignitaries at charity functions. All very staid and proper. The rest was all about your sporting triumphs. The romp in the fountain was a one-off.'

He looked away. 'Once was enough.' He dropped a couple of tea bags into cups and poured on the freshly boiled water. 'You disappeared. What then?'

She continued looking at him for a moment but he concentrated on the tea, avoiding her gaze, and she knew there was a lot more to the story than that but he wanted her story, all of it, so that there would be no more surprises.

'When I was twenty-one and had control of my inheritance I sold the family jewellery, added it to the money from the sale of the house and put it all into a fund for the women my father had robbed.'

'I don't imagine your lawyers were happy about that.' He didn't sound surprised. 'Did they try and stop you?'

'Yes, but I wanted an end to it, Bram. I kept the London flat because I needed somewhere to live, the family wedding ring that I wear, the pearls my mother was given on her eighteenth birthday,' she said, touching the single strand at her neck, 'and my great-great-great-grandmother's engagement ring. I got a job and got on with my life.'

'It was that easy?'

'Actually, yes. People go through the motions, ask the standard questions, but all they really want to talk about is themselves.' She looked up as he placed two cups of pale straw-colour liquid on the table in front of her. 'I appear to have overestimated the living-in-England effect.'

'It's camomile. It will help you sleep.'

He had more confidence in the calming power of herbal tea than she had, but she thanked him.

'There was no one close?' he asked.

'A relationship, you mean?' She pushed away

the bitter memory of betrayal and shook her head. If she couldn't trust someone with her life then it wasn't a relationship. 'This is the first time I've talked to anyone about this.'

'I thought Amanda Garland knew every detail,' he said, joining her on the sofa.

'She does, but not from me.' *Everything.* She had to tell him everything… 'I'd been at my first job for nearly a year when a girl I'd been at school with came to work in the same company. There was that same astonished, "*Jools?*" Within twenty-four hours everyone knew who I was.' She hadn't been sure which was worse, the faux pity or the prurient interest, but there had been worse to come.

'Ruby…' He sounded, looked so concerned that, without thinking, she reached out and put a reassuring hand on his arm.

'The man I worked for said that I'd done nothing to be ashamed of, that it would be a nine-day wonder and I should just keep my head down and ignore any comments.'

'You were that good, even then?'

'Attention to detail,' she said and then, remembering what had happened earlier, blushed. 'I imagine I get that from my father.'

'I'm guessing that didn't happen,' he said.

'No. Jeff…' She stopped. That part of the story had no relevance to what she was telling him. 'Someone I worked with phoned in the story and the following morning I was on the front page of the paper that had run the original exposé. It must have been a slow news day because they reran the whole story, updating it with the cost of everything I was wearing, the salary I was earning, how much the London flat was worth. How I was still living a life of luxury, unlike my father's victims.'

'I don't suppose they mentioned that you had given up most of your inheritance to repay them?'

'The Trustees complained to the PCC and they placed a small statement to that effect on page thirteen of the paper about two months later.' She held her finger and thumb a few centimetres apart to indicate the size of their retraction.

He let slip a word—clearly he had no love for the press—and then said, 'You were a victim too.'

'Not in the eyes of most people. I owned a valuable piece of real estate, had a decent job, good clothes… It was school all over again. I was a prisoner in my own flat, with the press camped out on the pavement, my phone ringing non-stop with hacks wanting my "story", photographs of me on horseback to demonstrate my privileged lifestyle all over the Net.'

'As if once in a lifetime wasn't enough.'

'Maybe if my father had been tried, gone to jail, but there was no closure…' She shook her head. 'I managed to slip out, took the train to the coast, walked along the pier—'

'No!' He took her hand from his arm and held it tightly, as if he would save her all over again.

'No!' She shook her head. 'No,' she repeated, wanting to reassure him. 'But for the first time I understood why my mother had chosen that way out. Her life, as she knew it, was finished and at that moment so had mine.'

'You shouldn't have been on your own.'

'I wasn't. A fisherman saw me looking into the depths and brought me a cup of tea from his flask. He didn't say anything, just stayed with me until I was ready to leave, then walked back along the pier with me and when he'd seen me safely back to solid ground went back to his rod.'

'Where did you go?'

'To Amanda. Her agency had placed me in my first job and she called me, left a message to get in touch. She found me somewhere to stay, helped me find a new home, coaxed me into a new look, a new identity and then found me a temp job in a one-man office.'

'That would be the very helpful stockbroker whose secretary was on maternity leave?'

'Yes.' She smiled, remembering how kind he'd been. Obviously he'd seen the papers, knew who she was, but he'd never said a word. 'I've worked for her agency ever since.'

'So where did Ruby Dance come from?' he asked.

'My great-great-great-grandmother,' she said, spreading her hand so that the half-hoop of rubies glowed with hidden fire in the soft light. 'She was a chorus girl back in the days when foolish young men drank champagne from their slippers.' She looked up, smiled at what was a happy memory. 'The foolish young man who married her was my great-great-great-grandfather.'

'And this is the ring he gave her, the one that you kept,' he said, taking her hand.

'She was wearing this ring in a portrait that hung in the gallery at home.'

'Do you look like her?'

'She was fair, but my mother said that I have her eyes.'

'Then I understand why your many times great-grandfather was prepared to defy convention and make her his wife.'

'I…' She swallowed, conscious that he was still holding her hand. 'You said you wanted an unsuitable wife, Bram, and you've got the real deal,' she said. 'No one will blame you for wanting to be rid of a woman who kept her past a secret. If Sheikh Fayad knew I'd kept this from you he'd tear up the marriage contract right now without a second's thought.'

'That is not going to happen. I still need a wife, Ruby. I still need you.'

She sat back, the niggle that had been poking

around at the back of her brain all evening finally coming to the fore.

'Are you sure about that?'

Bram instinctively tightened his grasp on Ruby's hand, sensing that she was about to slip away, disappear from his life as not once, but twice she'd disappeared from her own.

'It's a bit late to suggest another candidate.'

'Is it?' Her expression was grave, thoughtful. 'This is a foot in the mouth question, Bram, but I won't be doing my job as your PA if I don't ask it.'

His PA…

At some point during this extraordinary day he had stopped thinking of her as his personal assistant, stopped thinking about this as a business transaction and he tried to pin the moment down.

Had it been when Fayad, negotiating her dowry, had tackled the question of settlements for the children they would have? When, having placed a ring on her finger with the vow that they would be joined for ever, he'd touched his lips to hers and felt her lips tremble beneath his own?

Or was it that moment when he'd seen the blood drain from her face and, without a moment's thought, had said, 'My wife…'?

Her words brought him back to reality with a jolt but Ruby had never lost sight of reality. Having spilled out the nightmare that she'd lived through—that had changed her life for ever—she was still focused on the reason why she was there.

'Ask your question, Ruby,' he said and, unwilling to relinquish the intimacy that had grown between them, he added, 'Afterwards, if you need any help removing your foot from your mouth, I will do my best to help.'

She flushed. 'This is serious, Bram.'

Of course it was. She was always serious. Still punishing herself for something that was not her fault.

When, he wondered, was the last time she'd had any cap-over-the-windmill, let-your-hair-down fun? What would it be like to see her laugh out loud, let herself go without a care for what anyone else thought, without being afraid of being judged for enjoying herself?

When, for that matter, had he?

'I'm sorry, Ruby. Say what's on your mind.'

'Right…' She took a rather shaky breath. 'Are you absolutely one hundred per cent certain that Bibi has her heart set on a career in medicine?'

He frowned. 'Bibi?' That was the last thing he'd expected.

'How do you know that she has a place at Cambridge?' she pressed and this time it was her hand tightening around his. 'What I'm asking—' her eyes were velvet-soft, full of concern '—could it be that your brother invented her plea for help in order to get you to back off? Stay away.'

He'd been so sure that she was going to ask him to let her go so that she could slip out of sight, return to the hidden life she'd been leading until now. But she was still thinking of others. Thinking of him.

He was beginning to understand why a man like Jude Radcliffe had spoken so highly of her. She was not just clever, impressively cool—he couldn't think of another person who would have dared suggest such a thing to him—but totally selfless.

'So that he can hang onto the throne? Is that what you're suggesting?'

She nodded, almost as pale as when a chance encounter had exposed her true identity, and he lifted his free hand to her cheek. 'Have a care, Ruby Dance,' he warned. 'If you continue to demonstrate such acuity, such care for my well-being, I may not be able to let you go in the autumn.'

The heat of her blush seemed to flow through his hand, flood into his body and, without warning, the only thing on his mind was the kiss they'd shared, because she had been there with him in that lost moment and the memory of it was driving all his blood in one direction.

'Are you saying that I'm right?' she asked.

'No. But thank you for being brave enough to ask the question.'

'I think the word you're looking for is foolhardy.'

'I have the word perfectly,' he assured her and, fighting the urge to draw her close, sit quietly with her head against his shoulder, her dark curls soft against his cheek, he let his hand drop, stood up, turned away so that she should not see his arousal. She deserved better than that of him. 'It's been a long day and we have an early start tomorrow.' And before she could even think the question…

'I'll sleep in my dressing room.'

'Goodnight, Bram.'

'Goodnight, Ruby. Sleep well.'

He didn't move until he heard the bedroom door click quietly shut and then dragged a shaky hand over his face, waiting for the longing to subside. It was nothing. A reaction to the emotional minefield he was treading.

No man could spend so much time up close and personal with those eyes, that mouth, and fail to be affected.

Once tomorrow was over and they could get back to work everything would fall back into place. He turned away from the closed door and, needing a distraction, picked up his phone, checked for emails.

There were a dozen or so and he flicked down through them until, without warning, he was looking at the photograph that Violet had sent of the moment he'd kissed Ruby. Living the moment again—feeling the silkiness of her cheek beneath his fingers, the softness of her lips, hearing the smallest of sighs as what should have been the merest touch had become something deeper. Want, need, desire lighting a match in the darkness…

Violet had said, 'This one is just for you…' and she was right. It was not a photograph to put in a silver frame on top of the piano. It was a photograph that a man would keep close, look at when he was far from home and then he'd call to hear the voice of the woman he loved.

He tossed the phone aside. Dammit, he'd spent too long in his own company, been too long without a woman.

If they'd been at the fort he would have gone for a swim, slept in the stables on the pallet that Khal used when one of the horses was sick.

The welcome had been warm here in his cousin's palace but there was inescapable protocol, formality, the familiar suffocating confinement that had driven him to escape his father's palace when he was a boy, seeking the freedom of the souk. The freedom that he'd found flying headlong down the most treacherous ski-runs in the mountains of Europe and America.

None of that had changed but he would not lie to himself; if, at that moment, he'd been with

Ruby, her arms around him, escape would have been the furthest thing from his mind.

He retrieved the phone and tapped the name 'Juliet Howard' into the search engine, searched 'images' and there she was, sixteen years old, astride some seriously impressive horseflesh, laughing for the camera as she held aloft a trophy, her eyes alight with the joy of triumph.

There were other photographs that had appeared in an article on promising young riders. Her dark hair, longer then, loose about her shoulders and her face, still with the softness of youth, brimming with optimism as she stood beside the horse that everyone believed would take her to a gold medal. And then he was looking at her five years older, leaving her office hand in hand with a man who she was looking up at with the glowing smile of a woman in love.

Jeff…

The name had slipped out. She'd quickly changed it to 'someone I worked with' but this was the man who'd phoned in the story. Set her up.

The man who was quoted as 'shocked', had no idea who she was and felt 'utterly betrayed' by her deceit. The man who had destroyed her life for the second time.

When Ruby slowly woke to a soft pink dawn she did not need to get out of bed and check Bram's dressing room to know that she was alone in the apartment. When he was near the air seemed to vibrate with the power he generated; her skin was sensitive to his presence.

She slipped on a silk wrap and checked the sitting room, expecting to see Noor. The room was empty but a table had been set up and on a snowy cloth was a jug of orange juice, a pot of steaming coffee and, under covers, an array of delicious breakfast treats. Fresh figs, olives, tomatoes, yogurt, soft goat's cheese, preserves. She had just lifted the lid on a dish containing warm unleavened bread when she sensed Bram's presence and looked up.

He'd been running, his face, throat, arms slicked with sharp, fresh sweat. The air was thrumming with pheromones and while she was still trying to think of something to say he reached out, took a fig and bit into it. The juice gleamed on his lips and she thought she was going to melt into a puddle right there at his feet.

'Did you manage to sleep?' he asked.

'Sleep?' With the scent from the jacket he'd worn all evening and then placed around her shoulders filling her head? When every touch of his hand had left a warm tingle on her skin that nothing short of a cold shower would remove?

'You were forced to confront a lot of unpleasant memories last night.'

Oh, that...

'It can be hard to switch off,' he said, regarding her with concern.

She called her brain to attention. 'The camomile tea helped,' she lied. The bed had been remade with fresh linen, but it would have taken a bucket of the stuff to float her past the image of Bram casually creating a damp patch as he'd added one last detail to her effort to fake the scene. 'When do we leave?' she asked in an attempt to get back into PA mode.

'As soon as you're ready.'

'Twenty minutes?' she offered.

'Noor is supervising the removal of your wardrobe to the boat,' he warned her.

'I've managed to dress myself since I was four years old, Bram, but if I need help with a zip I know who to call,' she added, not bothering to hide her irritation.

His grin as he picked up another fig and backed into his dressing room caught her sideways.

'I could do it in fifteen,' Ruby muttered crossly when she could breathe again. 'Ten in an emergency.' She poured herself a cup of coffee, sliced a fig over some yogurt and carried them through to her dressing room.

Aware that she was still on show at the palace, she had been going to wear a simple—that would be designer simple—black suit with an ankle-length skirt that had been amongst the clothes sent up from the mall the day before, and her mother's pearls.

What Noor had laid out for her was a dramatic *salwar kameez* in a heavy dark blue silk, vividly decorated with the peacock tail appliqué and embroidery that was Princess Violet's trademark, and a fine silk chiffon scarf that had been embroidered in the same design. There was dark blue lace underwear, a pair of turquoise-blue suede flats and a featherweight silk *abbayah* to throw over everything to keep off the dust.

Her new make-up had been laid out on the dressing table, together with her brush and two jewellery boxes, one containing the diamond wedding ring that Bram had placed on her finger, the other a necklace and earrings of turquoises that exactly matched the appliqué on the outfit, the shoes.

It seemed very exotic for so early in the morning, but presumably princesses had to dress to a higher standard than the average PA. Not that she had any choice. The clothes that she had brought from England and the brand-new wardrobe that had arrived from the mall were all gone. It was the *salwar kameez* or nothing.

CHAPTER SEVEN

BRAM'S HEAVYWEIGHT EX-MILITARY patrol boat bypassed Umm al Basr's new marina with its sleek white yachts, expensive high-rise apartments, five-star hotels and shopping mall and edged into the old harbour.

They had left Ras al Kawi with Khal at the helm and Mina's sons on board as cook and crew.

The boat hadn't been fitted out in the luxury demanded by the average multimillionaire but Noor, doing her best to hide her disapproval at this form of transport when there was a perfectly good aircraft sitting on the tarmac, was hard at work turning the main cabin into a suitable bedroom for a princess.

The décor was functional rather than Hollywood but no expense had been spared when it came to communications.

There hadn't been so much as a wobble as Bram had video-conferenced with contacts in Hong Kong and Mumbai. This might be the day that Bram returned from exile, but his entire focus was on finalising deals, setting up meetings and she was still his temporary PA as well as his temporary bride.

The only distraction was the flash of the diamonds as she typed up notes. She had intended to remove her ring when she'd changed into a pair of lightweight trousers and a fine knitted top for the boat trip, but she'd felt self-conscious about removing it with Noor watching.

As the coastline of Umm al Basr appeared, Bram had gone up on deck. Certain that he would want to be on his own as he approached his home for the first time in five years, she made the excuse of calling Peter's mother to remain below.

Now, distracted by the shouting and clanging as they tied up, she gazed out of the porthole at a part of the city that didn't appear to have changed in a hundred years. There were dun-coloured walls, shops that were no more than rooms with wide double doors that opened onto the street, but where there would once have been camels and donkeys there were now luxury four-by-fours, huge American pickup trucks and sleek saloon cars with dark-tinted windows parked in every available bit of shade.

A port official waited while the gangway was lowered and then disappeared from view as he came aboard.

She reached for her bag, assuming that he would want to see her passport, but it was Bram who appeared in the doorway.

'Come,' he said. 'Walk with me.'

Ruby grabbed a couple of bottles of water from

the fridge and stuffed them in her bag, threw on her *abbayah* and joined Bram on the quayside.

He'd changed into a grey robe, wrapped a red and white checked *shemagh* around his head, but if he thought it would make him less noticeable he was mistaken. He held himself in a way that commanded attention and he set off across the quay at a quiet, steady pace, ignoring the traffic that seemed to give way to him.

He seemed disinclined to talk and she took her cue from him as they passed through a dim, cool fish market that was being washed down now that the early morning catch had been sold.

They went on through the vegetable market and then out into narrow, dusty streets where dice rattled and counters clicked as old men sat outside street cafés, drinking tea and playing a board game at lightning speed.

There were traders selling spices from huge bins, pots and pans of all shapes and sizes, stalls with piles of jeans and bolts of cloth in every imaginable colour.

She lingered for a moment to admire a heavy dark red brocade that would make a gorgeous jacket. Bram did not stop and she shrugged apologetically at the man and hurried to catch up as he turned into an area where tradesmen were working.

There was the smell of freshly sawn wood, hot

metal as a handle was welded to a pan and, in the dark recesses of his workshop, a blacksmith was sending showers of sparks into the hot gloom as he hammered on glowing iron.

Bram stopped at the entrance and the smith plunged the metal into cold water before looking up and calling out something in Arabic; she didn't understand the words but the mocking familiarity was unmistakable.

'He knows you,' she said.

'I used to escape from the palace and come here. No boring lessons, no one to shout if I got dirty, just the fun of pumping the forge bellows with Abdullah and, if his father was in a good mood, a chance to beat hot iron with a hammer we could hardly lift.'

'Boy heaven.' He turned and looked at her for the first time since they'd left the boat. 'What did he say to you?' she asked but, before he could answer, Abdullah, wiping his hands on a dirty rag, called out again.

'He said he heard that I was out of a job and he's looking for an apprentice. And he's offering tea.'

'Tea and a job offer. Go for it. I'll make myself scarce while you catch up on old times,' she said, thinking that she could go back and get some of that cloth. There were tailors working in little hole-in-the-wall shops that could run up a copy of a favourite jacket in hours and she wasn't going to be a princess for ever. Well, maybe for ever, but in a few months she'd be back in London, back on the temp roundabout where clothes had to be practical rather than exotic.

'Stay,' he said, catching her hand as she took a step back. 'We will stop to buy your cloth on the way back.'

'I wasn't…' She hadn't realised that he'd noticed. 'I don't want to embarrass your friend.'

'He will show his respect by acting as if you are not here.'

A boy fetched a chair, placed it in a quiet corner shielded from the street and wiped off the dust. She thanked him, sat down, sipped the sweet tea he brought her, asked his name, gave him the little box of mints she carried in her bag, let him take a selfie with her phone, took one of them both.

They were giggling at the result when Abdullah called him sharply and when she looked up she realised that Bram had been watching her. He turned back to his friend and they parted with a warm handshake.

True to his word, he retraced their steps, bargained with the stallholder for the brocade she had admired, then moved on without waiting for it to be cut, or paying for it.

'He will deliver it to the boat. Khal will deal

with it,' he said without looking back. 'How is Peter?' he asked when she had caught up with him.

'He's flying home tomorrow. I've organised a care package. Books, his favourite sweets, home visits from a sports masseur. If there's anything else...?'

'You have it covered,' he said as they walked on through the old part of the town, past ornate mosques with exquisitely tiled domes, ancient arches, huge carved doors that occasionally opened to offer a glimpse into a shaded courtyard.

No longer silent, he shared memories of truant days spent with the blacksmith, boat-builders and fishermen while his diligent brother stayed in the classroom and worked at his lessons.

'You were born to be a younger brother, Bram.'

'Feckless, irresponsible?' he suggested.

'Free.'

Free.

Bram stopped and looked down at this woman who knew when to be quiet but when she spoke went straight to the heart of what he was feeling.

She had swept down, unannounced, into his life, an angel on a rescue mission. Was capable of enchanting both princes and the small son of a blacksmith. Of enchanting him...

'How do you do that?' he asked.

Her forehead buckled in a frown. 'Do what?'

He shook his head and carried on walking, reverting to silence as he reconnected with his home.

Nothing had changed in this part of the city. There were children playing, stray dogs and skinny cats sloping in the shadows looking for scraps, a goat chewing on the remains of a cement bag and then, as they turned a corner, they were in a different world.

Before them lay the new city with its high-rise towers gleaming in the sun, the brilliant green of well-watered verges, trees and a square where a fountain cooled the air.

For a moment he paused, disorientated, then he headed for a bench in the centre of the square. 'I've walked you off your feet.'

'My feet are used to walking. I loved the chance to get a glimpse into your childhood, see the markets and the old part of the city.'

'Not this?' he asked, with a gesture that took in the concrete and glass surrounding them.

She glanced around, shrugged. 'It's very impressive, but it could be anywhere.' She opened her bag and handed him a bottle of water.

He took it, drained half of it in a swallow. '*Shukran.*'

'*Afwan,*' she returned and he realised he'd spoken to her in Arabic without thinking. And that she'd replied.

'Not just for the water. For understanding that I

did not wish to talk. For your kindness to Abdullah's son.'

'Again, welcome.' She took a sip of water from her own bottle. 'Has it changed much?'

'This—' he made a broad gesture taking into the square '—is unrecognisable.' He shrugged. 'Or maybe I wasn't looking. It was Hamad who saw the potential for tourism, trade, offshore banking. If he'd ever left his books to come to the smithy he would have been figuring out how it could be run more efficiently.'

'Is that what Abdullah told you?'

He turned and looked at her. 'He told me that there are new hospitals. That his daughters go to school.'

'Not his son?' she asked.

'Boys always had that privilege but it's a holiday today.'

'Because you are coming home?' she teased, her smile warming him in ways that the sun never could.

'The holiday is to celebrate my father's birthday.'

'Of course.' Her smile faded. 'I didn't mean to be flippant.'

'No.' Unable to retract the words, bring back the smile, he said, 'Abdullah told me that he has a new house built with the money flowing into the country. He said that people admire and respect Hamad for the changes he has pushed through.'

Ruby said nothing; she just put her hand over his, a silent gesture of understanding, compassion.

He'd told her that this was what he wanted and it was, but the reality had raised a confusion of emotions and, turning his hand around, he wrapped it around hers, glad that she was there.

For a moment neither of them moved, spoke, but simply sat there in the sun, their hands locked together. The temptation was to stay there all day, but it had been a long time since breakfast.

'Are you hungry, Ruby?'

She placed her free hand against her waist. 'You heard my stomach rumbling?' she asked, all mock shock horror. 'I hoped you'd think that was thunder.'

Bram, appreciating her attempt to lift his mood, played along. He glanced up at the clear blue sky, raised an eyebrow. 'You think it looks like rain?'

'I think,' she said, 'that I spotted a burger place over there.' And he discovered, as he looked back into silver-grey eyes that sparkled in the sunlight that it wasn't so hard to smile after all.

'One day married and you're fobbing me off with fast food?'

'When we get home I'll bake you a cake,' she promised.

Home? She was talking of the fort as home?

'What kind of cake?' he asked, as a world of

possibilities opened up before him. The loss of one life but the possibility of another.

'Lemon drizzle, Victoria sandwich. Ginger? You choose.'

'All of the above,' he said, as the image of them alone in the kitchen as she made him some classic English cake gave him a warm rush of pleasure. 'And you beside me on Rigel riding along the beach.'

She hesitated and he knew why. Riding had been her passion and it had been taken from her. He was determined that, whatever happened, she would not lose it again.

'Ride with me and I won't make you slaughter a goat.'

She laughed. 'That's an offer I can't refuse but maybe we should stick to something a little less messy for lunch? I don't know about you but I could do with some comfort food right now. I'll have mine with everything except the pickle, extra fries and a milkshake so cold that it will give me a headache.'

He shook his head, laughing despite the uncertainty of what lay ahead. 'Extra fries it is,' he said as he stood up and, her hand still fast in his, helped her to her feet.

For a moment it lay small and white against his calloused palm, the ring he'd placed on her finger flashing in the sunlight. Then the *abbayah* slipped from her hair and she lifted it away to tug it back into place.

She was so easy to be with. He'd lost count of the times he'd imagined his return to Umm al Basr, walking through the souk the way he had as a boy, reacquainting himself with the places he had loved, aware that much of it would be gone.

He had imagined himself alone but when the moment had come he had wanted Ruby at his side, walking with him. She had lost everything and he knew she would understand what he was feeling.

'What was here when you were a boy?' she asked as they walked towards the burger bar.

Bram looked up at the tall glass-fronted buildings skirting a square that had been laid out like an Italian piazza.

'The odd wandering goat,' he said. 'Scavenging cats. Sheep just off-loaded in the harbour and being driven along to the market. A camel or two. Donkeys.'

Umm al Basr had grown outwards and upwards, become greener, richer, glossier in his absence; it was a place where growing numbers of tourists came to shop in the designer boutiques in the mall, to camp in the desert and to soak up the winter sun on the unspoilt beaches.

He'd been aware it was happening—he'd followed the development of the city under his brother's guidance from a distance—but it had all happened without him and he felt like a stranger.

He pointed towards the mall. 'Over there were old go-downs used by the traders to store their goods. One had a pile of old track bought for a railway that was never constructed. Now Hamad is planning a tramline. Eco transport to cut down on pollution.' He looked around. 'The new marina was built on the site of a boatyard where for centuries craftsmen built dhows that crossed the Indian Ocean and sailed down the coast of Africa. That disappeared while I was away at school.'

'You were sent away?'

'My father understood that the future was global and he was keen that I had an international education. I went to schools in France, America, England, studied politics at Oxford.'

'Weren't you homesick?'

'I missed my family…' He looked at her. 'I missed my family but I made friends, was invited to their homes, skied with them, stayed at their cottages in France, their houses in the Hamptons, went shooting in Norfolk and Scotland…' There had come a time when he'd only come home for major holidays and even then it was under pressure from his mother to show his face. 'I loved Europe, America. The social life, the global culture. My friends were there. For a while I forgot who I was. My responsibilities.'

'What about your family, Bram? When did you see them?'

'After Oxford I bought a house in London and my mother, sisters, came to shop and see the latest shows so often that I saw more of them than I would have here in Umm al Basr.'

'And now?' she asked.

'I moved out of the house so that they could continue to use it but they always seem to find some reason to call me if I'm in London. A dripping tap. A door that sticks. Oddly, the problem has always resolved itself by the time I arrive.'

'That would be just in time for lunch or dinner?' she said, trying so hard not to laugh that he wanted to hug her, hold her, try a rerun of that kiss…

'What about your brother?' she asked.

'He did a business course at Harvard, but he hated every minute he was away from home. Even when he came to London it was for business—meetings with architects, engineers, bankers—and he never stayed a moment longer than he had to.' He made a broad gesture that took in the high-rise buildings around them. 'While I was playing,' he said, 'my brother was building the future. This is all his work.'

'So how does he feel about you coming back, Bram?'

'You still think he's trying to keep me away?'

She stopped. 'I think there's something you're not telling me.'

'It's complicated,' he said as the doors of the burger bar swished open, engulfing them in a rush of cold air.

'Life is complicated,' she said, letting it go. 'Carbs help.'

She helped, he thought. Straightforward, undemanding and, when she wasn't concentrating on keeping in place the mask she'd been wearing since her own world shattered, that hundred-watt smile slipped through and lit up his day.

Back on board, they settled in the big leather armchairs of the saloon, Bram's long legs stretched out in front of him, Ruby curled up with her feet tucked beneath her. Neither of them spoke until the burgers had been demolished and there were only a few fries left.

Ruby sucked the salty deliciousness from her right thumb, wiped her hands on a paper napkin and sighed. 'Eating healthy food is a very good thing,' she said, 'but there are days when only fat and salt will do.'

'I hope you brought your pretty tap shoes with you.'

He remembered? A ripple of pleasure warmed her. Not good… This might be a long run for a temp but it was a very short-term assignment for a wife. Forget the kiss…

'I'm afraid not,' she said, picking up the milkshake. 'I didn't think I'd be here for more than a few days.'

'You'll just have to come running with me.'

About to say running was very bad for the knees, she was assailed by the image of him that morning, his skin slicked with sweat…

'I…I…haven't got any shoes.'

'Not a problem. We can run barefoot on the beach. At the water's edge.'

'R-right.' She sucked hard on the straw and winced as the cold hit the middle of her forehead but it dealt with the assault of sensory images—his long feet, the muscles of his calves, thighs—that were scrambling all sensible thought. 'When are you going to the *majlis*, Bram?'

'We. You are coming with me.'

'Me?' Ruby stopped massaging the centre of her forehead. 'I thought those were men-only events.'

'As a rule they are, but there must be no doubt. I will have the falcon I've brought my father as a gift on my right arm and you on my left.'

Both of them scared spitless…

'You want your return to be as scandalous as your departure so that your father can never reinstate you as his heir?'

'Never say never, but Hamad has worked for this. Done all the right things. While I…' He shrugged.

'You are taking a risk, Bram.'

He shrugged. 'Taking risks is what I do. On horseback, on skis, in the market. Today I'm taking a risk that you are right and my father wants me home more than he wants me to succeed him.'

'No pressure, then.'

He smiled. 'You're not just a Garland Girl now, Ruby, you're a Garland Princess and you're going to have to live up to your billing.'

Her nerves hitched up a level. He was relying on her…

'Have you got a red dress?' he asked.

'Cut to the navel, slit up the side? Five-inch heels?' she asked. 'Do you really think that I'll need a scarlet woman dress to draw attention to myself?'

'No.' He looked at her for the longest moment before shaking his head. 'You'd cause a sensation if you were wearing a sack but I don't want you to look as if you're apologising for being there. Today is a triple celebration. My father's birthday, my return and my marriage. Wear something spectacular.'

The sun was setting as their limousine stopped at the entrance to the palace, where Noor and Khal were waiting. One or two people standing near the entrance to the palace glanced across as he got out but had already moved inside by the time he offered her his hand to help her from the car.

Noor immediately began fussing around her, rearranging the folds of her coat. It was heavy ruby-red silk, thickly embroidered and appliquéd in gold and worn over a floor-length full-skirted dress made from black silk chiffon that had a band of matching embroidery around the hem.

She straightened the ornate gold choker chosen from a chest containing tray after tray of jewels—Ruby didn't ask where they had come from, she didn't want to know. Finally, Noor draped a filmy red and gold scarf so that it covered her hair, carefully arranging the long tails that fell to the floor at her back.

'Eyes low, *sitti*,' she instructed, clearly not at all happy that her lady was being subjected to this shameful disregard for tradition. 'No smile.'

Bram, the falcon that was his gift to his father settled on his gloved hand, heard her and said something to her in Arabic. She shook her head but, after one last tweak of the scarf, she turned and walked away.

'What did you say to her?'

'To wait for you at the rear of the *majlis*. If things go well she will take you to my mother.'

'Right.' And that would be the good outcome.

She didn't ask what would happen if things did not go well.

'And forget what Noor said to you. Keep your head up, eyes front and ignore everyone but my father.'

Her heart was pounding, her mouth dry. This was breaking all the rules, a gamble. She had nothing to lose but for Bram it was everything and she had to get it right.

'Head up, eyes front. Smile or no smile?'

Bram had waited, delaying his arrival until everyone was there. The vast entrance lobby, fifty metres long and nearly as wide, was now busy with men who'd paid their respects, drunk coffee with the ruler and overflowed from the *majlis,* where they were talking with friends, discussing business, catching up with the gossip.

'Be yourself, Ruby,' he said as she rested her hand on his so that the diamond ring on her finger flashed in the light from the chandeliers. She was trembling, he realised, and he turned his hand so that his fingers curled around hers. 'Just be yourself.'

She swallowed but lifted her head and looked straight ahead.

Despite its vast size, there was no room to simply walk through and he paused in the doorway until someone, noticing them out of the corner of his eye, took a step back to let them pass, then did a double take at the sight of a woman and another as he realised who was standing beside her and nudged his companion.

There was a ripple effect as men turned and the loud burble of conversation gradually died away, leaving the room silent except for the rustle of shocked men stepping back, the pounding thud of his heartbeat…

'Bram?' Ruby murmured when, frozen to the spot, he could not move.

'This is like leaping out of the starting gate of the Lauberhorn,' he said softly. Two and a half heart-pounding minutes at over one hundred and fifty kilometres an hour on one of the most terrifying downhill ski runs in the world.

Ruby, who moments before had been shaking with nerves, gave his hand a reassuring squeeze and when he looked down at her she was smiling. 'Head up, eyes front,' she murmured. 'There is only one man here who matters.'

In that moment he knew that wasn't true; there was only one woman. Strong, brave, true…

Without a thought for where they were, the seriousness of the occasion, everything he was risking, he lifted her hand to his lips and the light from a dozen chandeliers caught the diamonds he'd placed on her finger and flashed a rainbow that lit up the room with colour. Or maybe it was just his life, he thought as he returned her smile, then looked to the front and took a step forward.

As they walked towards the *majlis*, the crowd closed in behind them, no one wanting to miss this. By the time they reached the great doors everyone was aware that something out of the ordinary was happening in the reception hall and the room was silent with expectation, all eyes turned towards them.

Another hundred metres, long seconds which gave his father, his open-mouthed brother and Ahmed Khadri all the time in the world to see the ring glittering on Ruby's finger, absorb the message he was sending, time to decide on their reaction.

At the foot of the dais he handed the falcon to a guard who, at a nod from his father, stepped forward to take it. Then, his hand free, he placed it on his heart, making a low bow as he wished his father a long life, good health, many grandsons. Before the Emir could respond, he added, 'I have another gift for you on your birthday, my lord. May I present to you Rabi al-Dance? A daughter for your house, the mother of my sons.'

He was glad that he was speaking in Arabic so that Ruby did not know what he was saying.

His father, having been given plenty of time to consider his reaction, said, 'There is a contract between you?'

'Written and sealed by Sheikh Fayad al Kuwani, Emir of Ras al Kawi. Rabi has no living family but Fayad stood for her in the matter of a dowry.'

'He was demanding?' he asked.

'He protected her interests as diligently as any father, my lord, but there will be no call on you.'

Ahmed Khadri remained stony-faced, his brother's eyebrows were through the roof, but his father came very close to smiling.

'Where will she live?' he asked. 'Your mother and sisters enjoy your London house.'

His father was negotiating with him?

He smothered any notion of smiling. 'It is my gift to them. I have my own apartment and my wife, as is her right, will have a house of her own.'

His father nodded, rose to his feet and stepped down to embrace him. He was shockingly older, thinner than on the day he had disinherited him, but his grip was still strong. 'It is good to see you here, my son. It has been too long.' He looked at him for a long moment then nodded before turning to Ruby. 'You are welcome, Umm Tariq,' he said in English—mother of Tariq—a message to those present that he had accepted the wife his son had chosen and that her first son would bear his own name.

Ruby, head bowed, made a deep curtsey. '*Shukran*, Your Highness. I am honoured to be here.'

His father took her hand and, with a smile,

urged her to her feet before turning to him. 'Take your bride to your mother, Ibrahim, and then come and sit with us.'

As he returned to his throne Hamad made a move to surrender his seat to his older brother but their father laid a hand on his arm, keeping him at his side, and Bram felt the tension slip from his shoulders. With that one gesture, his father had shown his people that while his oldest son had been welcomed back into the fold, Hamad remained his chosen successor—that the accord with the Khadri family would hold—and there was a shift in the air as a hundred men released the breath they had been holding.

Ahmed Khadri, meantime, had no choice but to surrender his own seat to make room for him but he took his time about it and, rather than move down the order of precedence, he sketched the merest nod at the throne, pausing beside him long enough to murmur, 'Take care not to turn the other cheek, Ibrahim al-Ansari. My knife will cut deeper.'

'It went well?' Ruby asked anxiously as he ushered her to a door at the rear of the *majlis* where Noor was waiting to escort her to his mother.

'It went well, thanks to you. My father not only signalled his acceptance of you but kept Hamad at his side, a clear indication to everyone present that he remains as heir.'

'And the man who left? That was Bibi's father?'

'Ahmed Khadri is no doubt on his way to inform her that I have disappointed another Khadri bride.'

She laid cool fingers against his cheek. 'That man hates you, Bram. Take care.'

He covered her hand with his, holding it against his face, resisting the urge to kiss her palm. 'It's in the past, Ruby.' Reluctantly, he let go of her hand and took a small battered wooden box from his pocket. 'Give this to my mother. And if you see Safia, tell her that her prayers have been answered.'

'Prayers?'

'She will understand.'

Noor led the way towards the back of the palace, quickly running through the formalities of meeting the woman who was not only her mother-in-law but an Emira. Then, as a pair of wide double doors opened before them, she curtsied low and stepped aside, leaving Ruby on her own.

The news had clearly preceded her. The Emira was standing in the centre of a large room with her daughters, daughter-in-law and countless other female relatives gathered protectively around her, while children crawled and raced around them, oblivious to the drama.

This was not like the *majlis* where, at Bram's prompting, she had kept her head up, eyes forward, facing down the men who would be shocked by her presence. This was a moment for submission. As the door closed behind her, head bowed, she curtsied low, murmured, 'Emira…' as she offered her the box that Bram had given her on outstretched hands.

There was a moment of breath-holding silence and then the Emira put her hand beneath hers and, with the slightest pressure, invited her to stand before she took the box and held it, gently rubbing her hand over its battered surface as if it was something much cherished.

'This,' she said in clear, barely accented English, 'was the first gift that my son gave me when he was four years old.' She lifted the lid of the box and inside, on purple velvet, nestled a piece of turquoise-blue sea glass that she lifted out and held against her lips for a long moment before looking up. 'We were walking on the beach and he saw it being turned at the edge of the water. He thought it was a jewel and he gave it to me in this little box. I sent it to him when he was banished, a piece of home to keep with him,' she said. 'My promise that one day he would return.'

She replaced the glass in the box, looked up and, with a smile, extended a hand. 'Welcome, Rabi. Come and meet your sisters.'

His four older sisters each kissed her on both cheeks, and then there was Safia with her new baby. She was extraordinarily beautiful, with blue-green eyes that shone from her lovely face as she stepped forward to kiss her cheeks, and when Ruby, very quietly, gave her Bram's message those eyes filled with tears.

Before she could speak, Ruby found herself swept away into a comfortable inner sitting room strewn with toys for the little ones who were being entertained by the older children. Mint tea and small sticky cakes were pressed upon her, along with a dozen questions. All the women spoke good English but, to her relief, the Emira was not interested in how she had met Bram.

Inventing a world class romance for Violet was one thing, but Bram's mother had the kind of eyes that missed nothing. As she brushed aside her daughters' eager questions and asked about her family and their history, Ruby had the feeling that she knew exactly what Bram had done.

Fortunately, her family had plenty of history and she kept them entertained with stories—tales that had no doubt grown taller in the telling—of ancestors who had served kings and queens throughout the centuries until, at last, a stir beyond the doors announced the arrival of their husbands.

Bram, his hand upon his heart, bowed low to his mother then enfolded her in a heartfelt hug before turning to his sisters and embracing them each in turn. Finally he turned to Safia, acknowledging her with a formal bow.

'Your sister is not with you, *sitti?*' he asked, speaking in English, in deference to her presence. 'I had hoped to congratulate her on achieving her heart's desire.'

'We are very proud of her,' she replied. 'Sadly, she has been confined to her room with a chill.'

'I hope she will soon recover. Please give her my wife's very best wishes for the future.'

'Thank you, *sidi*. She will be desolate to have missed such a glad occasion.'

There had been nothing to suggest it had been anything but the most formal exchange and yet Ruby had been aware of an undercurrent, a deeper layer of meaning.

She glanced at Hamad, but he, like the other men, had been surrounded by the little ones as soon as he'd arrived and, bending to pick up the little girl clutching at his knees, had not witnessed the exchange. Or had he turned away rather than see his brother greet the woman who should have been his bride?

A birthday supper was served with three generations of the family together, a chaotic, happy, noisy mix of children and adults. Everyone wanted to talk to Bram, hug him, welcome him. And if Safia slipped away early looking pale, everyone understood that she had been unwell, needed rest.

Ruby, watching her leave, certain that there was more to her pallor than a difficult childbirth, jumped as Bram put his hand on her shoulder. He gave her a wry smile as she turned to him and bent to whisper in her ear, 'You're supposed to melt when I touch you, not jump.'

Which was all very well for him to say, but ever since that kiss it was as if she'd been wired up to jump leads—one touch and her feet left the ground—but, aware that they were the centre of attention, she whispered, 'So messy, melting…'

'Rabi—' Fathia and Nadiya converged on her, grinning as they shooed Bram away. 'Come and sit with us,' Fathia said, taking her hand and leading her towards a sofa. 'We want to hear exactly how you met Bram.'

'And how you got a man who swore he would never marry to put that gorgeous ring on your finger,' Nadiya added.

Swore never to marry? She turned, met his gaze and Bram shrugged.

'She's the best temporary PA in London,' he said. 'Hugely in demand. The only way I could ensure she stayed was to marry her.'

'You expect her to work for you?'

'Of course. In fact, I have a pile of emails that

need attending to,' he said, disengaging her from his sisters. 'We have to go.'

Shocked, Nadiya said, 'But that's—'

'He's teasing,' Fathia said, grinning. 'Let them go.'

'Oh…' Nadiya blushed.

'Tomorrow,' Fathia said, smiling, 'we'll pick you up and take you shopping for honeymoon clothes while Bram spends the morning talking politics with Abbi and Hamad.' She leaned forward and in a loud mock whisper said, 'We'll have lunch and you can tell us *everything*.'

CHAPTER EIGHT

'THANK YOU FOR rescuing me from the third-degree back there.'

'A brief postponement, no more,' Bram said as, hidden within the dark-tinted windows of the limousine, they were driven back to the harbour. 'I thought you might welcome a break.'

After dinner there had been a seemingly endless round of visitors who wanted to welcome him home. Congratulate him on his marriage. Wonderful though it had been to see everyone, he was glad to escape to the peace and quiet of the boat.

To be alone with Ruby.

'I had a practice run with Violet and Leila,' she assured him. 'Your mother stepped in before your sisters could get started but if by "everything" they mean what I think they mean I'm going to need time to get my imagination in gear.'

'Just say if you need a refresher course.'

He anticipated one of her smart rejoinders but instead she caught her breath, lowered her lashes, turned to look out of the window and, without warning, he was the one struggling to breathe.

'Ruby...'

'I think I can remember the basics,' she said as she turned back to face him, breath almost back to normal, but her eyes, dark and deep as space, betrayed her. He was not alone… 'Your mother, I'm happy to say, was more interested in my antecedents than how we met.'

Melt… He'd told her she should melt but right now he was the one in meltdown, longing to hold her, kiss her, once more taste those lovely lips. Every cell in his body was responding to the look in her eyes. She was fighting it and he'd made her a promise but he was the one taking a slow, steadying breath before he said, 'My mother was ignoring the fact that we should not have met without her approval.'

'And family is far more important than romance. I understand that. Fortunately, although I'm short of the living variety, I do have centuries of ancestors to call on.'

She pulled at her lower lip with her teeth and he felt a more urgent tug of heat…

'I'm afraid I dropped names left, right and centre.'

'Names?' he repeated, hanging onto reality by a thread.

Her smile widened. 'You don't hang onto your estates through war and revolution for as long as our family did without making yourself useful to whoever wears the crown. My three times great-grandfather might have raised eyebrows with his chorus girl bride but his son was an aide to King George V.'

He tried to concentrate on what she was saying, but all he could think of was how her mouth had tasted. How it could become an addiction…

'Impressive. Safia—' *think of Safia* '—must have been praying very hard for you to have walked into my life at the exact moment I needed you, Ruby.'

'I gave her your message.' She frowned and he barely restrained himself from reaching out to smooth it away.

'What did she say?'

'Nothing. She was just shocked, I think, but she didn't have time to say anything before I was grabbed by your sisters.' She looked up. 'I won't be able to lie to your mother, Bram. If she asks me the direct question.'

'If she asks you the direct question do not hesitate to tell her the truth,' he said, reaching for her hand, meaning only to offer a reassuring touch, but somehow it was curled into his, a perfect fit.

'She'll be terribly shocked.'

'On the contrary. She will tell you that all great marriages are arranged for the good of the family and the state. The fact that we arranged it ourselves may be unconventional, but the result is the same.'

'Hardly great. It's going to be the shortest marriage in the history of Umm al Basr.' Was that regret? 'Perhaps I should have told her about my parents. Made myself a little less suitable so that she'll be relieved when you divorce me. But I wanted your homecoming to be a happy day.'

'Then you achieved your wish.'

He'd sat with his family, enjoying the teasing conversation that he could only have with those who'd known him from a baby, but his eyes had been constantly drawn to Ruby.

She'd fitted in so easily. He'd watched as one of his nieces clutched at her knees with sticky fingers. Totally unconcerned about her dress, Ruby had lifted her onto her lap for a cuddle, accepted a wet kiss, pretended to nibble on the half eaten biscuit the infant had thrust at her.

His mother, catching his eye, had smiled her approval and he had felt his wizened heart, so long deprived of all he loved, expand and fill with longing for this to be real.

Only Safia, unconvinced, had been quiet, distant, excusing herself early to see to her baby. She'd caught his eye once, a desperate, what-have-you-done? question blazing out of her eyes, but then only she and Hamad knew that he had been warned. Suspected that this marriage was a sham.

'Your mother showed me the sea glass,' Ruby said. 'She told me how you put it in your treasures box and gave it to her when you were a little boy.'

'Did she tell you what she wrote when she sent

it to me?' She nodded, her eyes suddenly liquid. 'Is that a tear?' he asked.

'Just a little one,' she said, blinking hard but failing to catch it. Touched by this evidence of her empathy, he took his hand from her and wiped the stray tear from her cheek with the pad of his thumb, before cradling her cheek as if it was the most natural thing in the world. Because it was.

For a moment she continued to look up at him, eyes glistening, her mouth temptingly soft, with only an anxious little frown to mar the smooth perfection of her skin. He wanted to kiss it away, reassure her, tell her that she'd been amazing. That he couldn't imagine a more suitable wife if his mother had lined up every single one of the well-born daughters of Umm al Basr for him to choose from.

The way she'd walked beside him through the *majlis,* had spoken to his father. She'd been like a rock at his side…

'You should have given it to her yourself but it was a clever move,' she said. 'It got us both over that first awkward moment.'

'That was my intention,' he said, lifting his arm and putting it around her, drawing her close. She didn't resist, but let her head rest against his shoulder. No doubt she was tired. She couldn't have slept much for the last two nights and it had been another long day.

'How was your father?' she asked.

'In very good spirits. He's brought me home without having to submit to the Khadris' demands—' in private the old man had scarcely been able to contain his delight at besting his old enemy '—and he's anticipating the swift arrival of a grandson to keep them out of the succession altogether.'

He saw the gentle ripple of her throat as she swallowed. 'I'm sure, given time for Safia to recover, your brother will do his best to ensure that doesn't happen.'

'That would be the diplomatic solution,' he agreed, 'and my brother is nothing if not a diplomat.'

'And he has a three-girl start on you.' She looked up at him, looked away again quickly but not before he saw the tinge of pink darken her cheeks. 'So today went as well as you could have wished,' she said quickly.

Not exactly, he thought, as her hair brushed against his cheek. His plan had been very simple. A paper marriage and a swift divorce. The marriage had succeeded beyond his wildest dreams but every minute he spent with Ruby made the divorce part of the deal less and less appealing.

'Everyone is happy,' he assured her.

'Except the Khadris.' She gave a little shiver and he drew her closer.

'They'll get over it.'

'What about you, Bram?' She turned her head to look up at him. 'Are you happy?'

'Happy… That's a very shallow word to describe the way I'm feeling at this moment.'

Sitting with his arm around this amazing woman… There was only one thing that would make him happier, but there was no rush. He had until the autumn to make their legend, all those stolen moments they had invented, a reality. To convince her to stay.

'I was happy when I escaped the palace as a boy, playing polo, risking my neck on ski runs.' Right now he felt as if he was on the verge of something new, life-changing. 'Maybe I was born too late. As a young man my grandfather was battling the Khadris for grazing and water, protecting our traditional fishing grounds and pearl beds from their raiding parties, stealing their daughters.'

'So you looked for other ways to risk your life. Will you go back to the mountains now you've served your penance?' she asked.

'It's been too long. Downhill racing demands total dedication.'

'I don't understand why you gave it up.'

'Don't you? You gave up riding. It wasn't just the press, was it?'

She shook her head. 'I'd lost everything I cared about. I had no heart for it.'

'But you will ride Rigel?'

'Will you ski for fun?'

He'd never thought of skiing as anything other than a demanding sport but the idea of fooling around in the snow with Ruby was very appealing and she hadn't had any fun in a long time. 'It's getting a bit late in the season, but maybe we could spend the New Year in Switzerland?'

He held his breath, waiting for her answer.

'Skiing is just an expensive way to break a leg,' she said. 'Besides, you'd be bored to death teaching a falling-down beginner.'

'Picking you up will be a great deal more enjoyable than avoiding once-a-year skiers on crowded slopes.' She hadn't reminded him that the cut-off date for their marriage deal was September. She hadn't said no… 'However, for a woman expected to win equestrian gold at the Olympics, you appear to have a very high aversion to risk.'

'Or maybe a well-developed sense of self-preservation.'

'We can stick to making snowmen until you're begging to get out on the slopes.' He held his breath.

'Snowmen I can do.'

'In the meantime, how do you feel about scuba diving?'

'Scuba diving? That's not in the job description,' she said.

'Your job description, as I recall, is "whatever is necessary". Right now that's being my bride, and my sisters all wanted to know where I was taking you for our honeymoon.'

'And you told them you were going to dress me up in rubber and take me underwater?' she mocked, but he knew now why she did not like the sea. 'What did they have to say about that?'

'When I told them I was taking you to the Maldives they all just sighed. However, since there's nothing to do there but lie in the sun and make love, I thought perhaps we would need a distraction.'

'No…'

She struggled to sit up but his arm was about her waist and her weight against him was a pleasure gained that he was unwilling to relinquish.

'You would not be alone, Ruby, staring into the cold water of the North Sea, betrayed by the man you loved, your life in shreds. Your hand will be in mine as we swim in the warm blue waters of the Indian Ocean,' he said, 'and I will keep you safe.'

'Bram…' Her eyes were troubled, her lips trembling.

'I saw the picture of you outside your office with the man you could not bring yourself to tell me about. He was pointing at something so that you would be looking across the street, into the lens of the photographer who was lying in wait for you, but you were looking up at him. Had eyes only for him.'

'Jeff.' She swallowed. 'He'd been at a client site that day but someone called to warn him what was going around the office and he'd found the story on the Internet. He thought he knew me, Bram—'

'Don't make excuses for him, Ruby. No matter how angry he was, a man with any kind of a backbone—'

'Bram.' His name was so soft on her lips that it felt like a newly minted word and as she looked up at him, took her hand from his and laid it against his chest, the breath caught in his throat. 'I've seen how a man with backbone reacts when confronted with an unexpected revelation. How he stands by her. Protects her.'

'*Ya habibati*,' he murmured, completely undone. '*Ya rohi…*'

The kiss—so wrong, so right—was a breath away. A hand slipped to her neck, his fingers tangling in her hair. He could feel her breath on his lips…

'Workplace relationships are never a good idea,' she said, holding him off.

'I could fire you.'

'Or I could resign.'

'I accept,' he said, lowering his lips to hers, with the same nervous uncertainty of a boy kissing a girl for the first time. He was shaking with the hugeness of it, the knowledge that nothing would ever be the same again. That he would never be the same…

Her lips were soft, yielding sweetly until, catching her breath, she drew back a little to look at him, her eyes molten silver, black velvet, searching his face.

Trust me…

His head was booming with the words and he wanted to shout them to the skies, but they were hollow, meaningless in the heat of desire. They were spending so much time together, sharing secrets, growing closer but trust was something that had to be lived every day, every hour, every minute.

There had been moments when it would have taken no more than a look, a touch to ignite the tension that sizzled between them, set it ablaze. Always conscious of the deal they had made, he'd taken a step back and he would do it again and again for as long as Ruby needed to trust him, trust herself…

Ruby had been so certain that she could do this. She'd shied away from the possibility of any kind of entanglement for so long that, despite the undeniable attraction, she was sure she could play the part of Bram's wife for his family, for all the world, while keeping her distance in private.

She had been fooling herself.

The knee-melting heat of desire had been there in that first shocked moment when he'd appeared wearing nothing but a towel and, dry-mouthed, she'd watched water trickle down his broad golden chest. When she'd stumbled on the steps and breathed in the warm male scent of his body as he'd caught her, held her. In that moment when she'd been unable to stop herself from reaching up to touch the scar on his cheek.

He'd taken her hand then and it had felt like a perfect fit.

She knew it was the intimacy of co-conspirators that made the air thrum with tension when they were in the same room. That the only reason he caught her eye to share a private smile, touched her shoulder as he passed, was to convince the world that they were a couple. But the wedding had felt so real. His kiss had felt so real.

Now he was talking about a honeymoon, about keeping her safe. And he was kissing her, not like a man confident of his power but a man for whom this was the most important moment in his life. Giving her time to choose where this would go. Step out of the shadows and take the risk…

With no secrets between them, nothing hidden, she closed her hand over his robe, bunching it in her fist, closed her eyes and said, '*Ya habibi.*'

His hand, cool, gentle, cradled her face. His lips brushed her eyelids, her cheek, and as they touched her mouth she felt herself melt against him, boneless, holding her breath, waiting for more, desperate for more. He took his time, cradling her head, his thumb against her jaw, his finger sliding through her hair, tilting her head back, brushing against her neck.

He paused to look down at her for a long moment before taking the kiss to another dimension; his tongue sliding over her lower lip before slowly, thoroughly, he took possession of her mouth, lighting up all the longing, need, that she'd suppressed for so long.

It was the impatient hooting of dozens of car horns that finally broke through the mist of desire and Bram drew back a little, kissed her again and then reached for the intercom switch. He exchanged a few words with the driver and then said, 'Someone's been rear-ended. It will be hours while they argue who's to blame.'

'Hours?'

'You're in a hurry to get somewhere, *ya habati*?'

He didn't wait for an answer but opened the door and they tumbled out, laughing, as they began to run, dodging around the cars until they reached the harbour.

The gangway bounced beneath their feet as they ran up it and then, as soon as they were aboard, he pulled her into the dark shadows of the bulkhead, took her in his arms. 'Are you sure about this, Ruby?'

'*Ya habibi...*'

'Ruby… My soul… My life…'

There was a slow, continuous beeping noise, the familiar hospital smell and wooziness as she surfaced from unconsciousness. Panic…

'Daisy,' she croaked. 'Is Daisy hurt?'

'Ruby…'

She opened her eyes, saw Bram, felt his hand, warm and strong, in hers and, certain that she would be safe, she let the darkness drag her back.

'Has she come round?'

Bram looked up as his mother reached his side, put her hand on his shoulder. 'She stirred a while ago.'

'She is strong. She will live to bear you many children.' She bent and kissed him. Kissed Ruby.

The beeping was back, insistent, annoying. Ruby wanted to tell someone to turn it off but when she opened her eyes the light was so bright that she closed them. Then opened them again. She had not been mistaken. Bram was on his knees beside her, his forehead resting against their joined hands, whispering words that she did not understand.

'Bram?' She made the words with her lips but there was no sound. 'Bram…' she repeated, trying harder. Her voice sounded rusty and it hurt her chest when she tried to catch a breath but he raised his head and she saw that his eyes were sunken, with dark shadows beneath them.

'Ruby.' Her name was layered with exhaustion, relief, emotions that she was too tired to unravel. 'Ruby, my soul, my life, how can you ever forgive me?'

Forgive him? What had he done?

'Could I have some water?'

He poured a little water into a glass, supporting her head as he touched it to her lips so that a little trickled into her mouth.

'Thank you.'

'Don't.' He looked as if he was the one in pain. Was he? Had he been hurt? 'Don't thank me.'

'I'm in hospital…' That beeping was a machine measuring out her vital signs. 'What happened to me? Was there an accident?' She tried to sort through the jumble of images in her brain. 'We were in the car.' She remembered a kiss. Or had she dreamed that?

'There was a hold-up. A collision at the entrance to the harbour.'

'Yes.' She remembered the blaring horns.

'You're smiling.'

'Yes.' The kiss had been real. But then… 'We were running.' Running, laughing as they'd run back to the boat, laughing as he'd drawn her into the shadows, unable to wait another moment to touch each other, hold each other. 'You asked me if I was sure.' She frowned. 'What did I say?'

'You don't remember?'

She remembered his arm about her waist, his fingers in her hair, the scent of steel and salt water and oil. The darkness of Bram's eyes, the anticipation of a kiss that would change her world and then something else. 'There was someone in the shadows. I saw a flash…'

'You saved my life, Ruby.' His hand tightened over hers. 'You cried out and, as I turned, Ahmed Khadri's knife missed me and hit you below the collarbone. You've lost a great deal of blood but there is no permanent damage, *insha'Allah*. If you had been taller…' He caught himself as if simply saying the words was to tempt fate. 'This is my fault. I should have stayed away.'

'There is only one person to blame.' She felt like lead, her shoulder was aching and the anaesthetic lingering in her bloodstream was dragging at her eyelids. 'The man with the knife.'

'You warned me. I did not listen.'

'Did he hurt you?' she asked.

He shook his head. 'When he saw what he had done he dropped the knife. I was yelling at him to call an ambulance while I tried to staunch the bleeding but he just stood there, useless for anything, but Khal heard me.'

'Where is he now? Ahmed Khadri?'

'He is at the *majlis*, waiting for the Ruler's justice. Waiting for my justice.'

'Your justice?' Woolly-headed, it took her a moment to realise what that meant. 'No!' She tried to sit up but she was hampered by wires hooking her up to the machinery and an IV tube in her hand. 'No, Bram…'

He caught her as she tried to pull them away, sending the machine into a frenzy, held her against his chest for a moment before easing her back against the pillow. Brushing her hair back from her face, he said, 'Who is Daisy?'

'Daisy?' she repeated, distracted.

'You asked about her.'

'Daisy was the first pony I rode in competition. I was over-ambitious at a jump, she dumped me in it and I broke my collarbone.'

'Was she hurt?'

'No. Bram—'

'The nurse is here to sort you out,' he said but, aware that he had attempted to distract her, she hung onto his sleeve, coughing in an attempt to clear her lungs of the anaesthetic, pull herself up…

'Don't do it, Bram.'

He did not pretend not to know what she meant. 'It's what he would do in my place.'

'You are not like him.'

'You do not know me,' he said, his face expressionless as, with a formal little bow, he backed away.

'You will start a war. Undo everything you sacrificed yourself for.'

'Some things cannot be left unanswered. I'll send Noor to you.'

'I know you!' she shouted after him. 'Bram!' But it was a doctor who appeared, a starched white coat over her sari, a jangle of bracelets at her wrist.

'Please, Princess, calm yourself or you will undo all my good work.'

'I have to get out of here.'

'We'll have you out of bed this evening and see how you feel then. Maybe you can leave tomorrow. You will be well cared for at the palace.'

'Not tomorrow. Now.' Ruby began pulling off the pads connecting her to the machine, holding out her hand with the IV to the nurse who had been attempting to reattach them. 'Remove this, please.' The nurse looked at the doctor but Ruby didn't wait for them to gang up on her. 'You do it or I will.'

The doctor lifted her eyes to the ceiling but nodded to the nurse.

'Where are my clothes?'

'*Sitti?*' Noor appeared in the doorway, white-faced, shaken. 'I heard the alarms…'

'It's nothing. I need my clothes. And a car. I have to see the Emira.'

'She said she would come back later—'

'Now…' It didn't come out as the sharp command she'd intended but Noor was already rushing to her side to support her as she slid her feet over the side of the bed, holding her until the room stopped swimming.

'You should lie down, *sitti*.'

'Ruby. Call me Ruby…' Still hanging onto the night table, she pulled herself upright. 'Have I got any clothes or will I have to go to the palace with my backside hanging out?'

Noor helped her out of the hospital gown and into a nightdress and wrap she'd brought from the boat. Wrapped her in her own *abbayah*.

A wheelchair was summoned and by the time they were at the door a car was waiting with Khal at the wheel.

Ten minutes later they were at the entrance to the family quarters of the palace.

'Khal, find Bram and tell him I want to see him

now. Immediately. Do you understand? Noor, take me to the Emira.'

'Rabi!' The Emira stood as Noor pushed her into the sitting room, filled with the same women who were there yesterday when they had been strangers. His sisters, Safia, all looking grave. No children.

'You have to stop him, my lady,' she said without ceremony. She had no strength to waste on unnecessary words. 'Please.'

The Emira rapped out words in Arabic, hands caught her as she slipped sideways, lifted her gently onto a sofa. A blanket was wrapped around her. The sharp, head-clearing scent of smelling salts was waved beneath her nose.

'Rabi…' Safia knelt beside her. 'Can you ever forgive me?'

'You wanted to help your sister.'

'No. Before that. Long before that.' She looked across to the Emira. 'The last time that Ibrahim came home, when you sent for him to make the wedding arrangements he saw…'

'Saw what?' she asked sharply.

'He saw that I loved Hamad.'

The Emira said something, sank into a chair.

'We were never alone, *sitti*,' she said quickly. 'We never did anything that you would disapprove of, anything shameful, but I spent so much time at the palace with you, learning how to be an

Emira, that I knew him like a brother. He cared for me like a brother. Never angry, always kind, always there. Ibrahim was a stranger.'

'What did he see?' the Emira demanded.

'Ibrahim saw me look at his brother, saw that there were tears in Hamad's eyes. That was all.'

'And he left without a word, without signing the contract.'

'He gave Nadiya a note for me. She thought it was a love letter but he said that when Hamad and I had looked at one another it was as if we were the only two people in the room. He said he would remember that look all his life.'

Unaware that behind her, in the doorway, Bram, Hamad and the Emir were listening, she said, 'He said he would fix things so that I could marry Hamad.'

'Safia…' Hamad crossed to her, held her, then turned to his father. 'Ibrahim staged the incident in the fountain, arranged for someone to film it and put it on the Internet, to call the police and the press in full knowledge of the consequences.'

'When you're faking a scene you have to pay attention to detail,' Ruby murmured as Bram crossed to her, took her hand. 'You are so good at the details.'

'Hush, *ya rohi*.'

'I did not know what he'd done,' Hamad continued. 'I believed he had dishonoured the woman I loved. I was the one who cut his face.'

There was an audible gasp from the Emira and her daughters.

'I would have told you the truth years ago,' he said, 'but Bram forbade it.'

'And Ahmed Khadri let everyone believe that he was the hero who'd avenged his daughter's honour?' Hasna gave a snort of disgust. 'What a loser.'

'My son—' his father took Bram's hand '—if I'd known…'

'If you'd known you would have been in an impossible position. I knew what I was doing. I'd do it again.'

'What can I do?' he said.

'Give me a moment alone with my wife.'

The Emira cleared the room with a gesture. 'Just a moment, Ibrahim. Ruby is exhausted.'

He nodded, then, as the door closed, leaving them alone, he knelt beside her, took her hand. 'I left you safe in hospital.'

'You left before I had finished talking to you.'

'Shouting at me,' he said, but he was smiling. 'You sounded exactly like a wife.'

'I sounded like a woman who was afraid that you'd do something you would regret.'

'If I'd had a knife in my hand when he struck you, I would certainly have killed him where he stood, but in cold blood? He expected it but it seems, *ya habati,* that you do know me.'

'Yes, Bram. I know you.' The painkillers were wearing off and the dull ache in her shoulder had sharpened into something darker. 'What will happen to him?'

'The court will decide on his punishment.'

'Well, good.' She coughed, winced.

'Your hand is freezing,' he said, rubbing it between his to get some warmth into it. 'I have to get you back to the hospital.'

'No.' She shook her head, wished she hadn't. 'I want to go home, Bram.'

'You'll have to wait until you're strong enough to travel to the fort.'

'Not there.' She was feeling faint, knew that she wouldn't be able to talk for much longer, but this was important. 'Not there. I want to go home to London. To my flat. It's over, Bram. You are back with your family. You don't need me any more. Tell them the truth. Annul the marriage.'

'You must rest. We'll talk when you're stronger.'

'No!' She tried to tighten her grip on his hand, but the message wasn't getting through and he tucked it beneath the blanket. 'You don't have to explain, Bram. I understand.'

She'd wondered why Safia was so certain that he'd stay away from his father's birthday *majlis*, give up the chance to return home, give up everything that mattered to him for her sister. She knew because he'd done it for her and there was only one reason a man would do that for a woman—because he loved her more than life itself.

'I knew there was something off about that scene in the fountain.' She was struggling to keep her eyes open. 'It was out of character.'

'And last night?' His voice was barely audible above the thrumming in her ears. 'What was that?'

Last night. When he'd kissed her and all the barriers she had built around her had come crashing down.

'That was…'

A dream, a moment when she had thought her world had been turned the right way up. A fantasy.

'That was just…' She gave up the struggle to keep her eyes open—it was easier to lie when she wasn't looking at him. 'Just sex.'

'Just sex?' Bram thumbed away the tear that had spilled down her cheek, gently kissed her cheek and pulled the cover up to her chin as the door opened behind him.

The doctor rested the back of her hand against Ruby's forehead, checked her shoulder. 'The wound has reopened, Sheikh. We need to get her back to the hospital.'

* * *

'The doctor told me that you've been asking her when you can leave,' Bram said.

'They've been wonderful, Bram.' Ruby was standing at the window, looking out over the sparkling blue water of the Gulf, not trusting herself to look at him. 'You've all been wonderful, but I'm ready to go home.'

He joined her at the window and the sleeve of his robe brushed against her arm as he stood beside her. 'We will stay here until you are stronger.'

She had expected that, prepared herself. 'No—'

He turned to her. 'You are determined to return to London?'

His expression was unreadable. It had been unreadable since she'd lost consciousness on the sofa in his mother's drawing room. Since she'd denied that there had been anything between them but a rush of emotion-fuelled lust.

Just sex…

His close-cut beard had grown, there were shadows beneath his eyes and his cheeks were hollow. She'd told him that he looked a wreck, worse than she did, but he had been stubbornly deaf to her plea for him to go back to the palace and rest.

For two days she'd drifted in and out of consciousness but every time she'd opened her eyes he had been in the chair at her side or wrapped in a cloak lying on the floor beside her bed, waking the moment she stirred.

In the week that followed he'd had food specially prepared for her at the palace, brought little treats to tempt her to eat. He'd been attentive, endlessly caring, always there and yet as distant as a star.

He had not touched her, not even to hold her hand. Had not murmured soft Arabic endearments that she did not understand. Why would he?

There was no further need to pretend that this was anything but an arrangement that had run its course. It was guilt, duty, honour that was keeping him a prisoner at her side and if she had learned anything from him it was that when you loved someone you let them go.

She lifted the arm that had been pinned up in a sling. 'I'm not going to be much use to you as a PA, Bram.'

'As I recall,' he said, 'I fired you.'

'Rubbish. I resigned.'

For a moment she struggled to keep the mask in place, act as if that kiss had never happened, keep it strictly business. 'I'll ask Amanda to send you a replacement.'

'You think that anyone could replace you?' His face, voice, remained unreadable.

'Please…' There was a lump in her throat as big as a rock and she had to swallow hard before she could carry on. 'You are home. Reconciled with your father. You need to move on.'

'While you run back to your hiding place?' he asked, a flicker of annoyance breaking through.

'No. I've had a lot of time to think in the last few days, Bram. I've been looking at courses on the Internet.'

'Courses?'

'I'm going to train as a riding instructor.'

His face softened. 'Reclaiming a little of your past.'

'No. I'm not looking back, Bram. I'm building a new future and I have you to thank for the courage to do that.'

'I suppose it's pointless asking you to stay at my house, where there are people to take care of you until you are fully recovered?'

'That's very generous of you, but I want to be in my own home.' She needed to have her familiar things about her. Get back to normality.

'If that is what you wish, I have to honour it. My plane is at your command.' He turned back to the window, the distant horizon. 'I regret that if you insist on leaving today I will not be able to travel with you. The Emir has summoned his Council and has asked me to attend.'

'Then you must,' she said. 'This is why we went through this, Bram. So that you can be here to support him.'

'Yes.'

'Will you tell them the truth?' she said.

'About you?' He looked at her then and for the first time in days he was smiling. 'Yes, Ruby, I will tell them.'

'And you will arrange for the marriage to be dissolved?'

'Fayad sent a copy of the contract to your lawyer, with an English translation. My lawyers will deal directly with them. Being lawyers, they will no doubt take their time. You are not in any hurry?' he asked. 'Our agreement was until September.'

'September will be fine.' Pointless to regret the promised New Year in the snow.

He nodded. 'Noor will travel with you and there will be a car to meet you.'

She considered telling him that she would take a scheduled flight, that she did not need a companion, that she could arrange her own car, but since she'd be wasting her breath all that remained was to thank him.

'*Shukran*, Sheikh Ibrahim. *Ma'al-salaama*.'

There was the faintest hint of a smile as he lifted his hand to his heart and with the slightest of bows said, '*Afwen, sitti. Ila-liqaa.*'

Bram's sisters kissed her and said they would see her when they were in London.

Safia brought Bibi to meet her. She seemed unbelievably young but happy to be leaving for England and university within the next few weeks.

Ruby wished her luck but as they left Safia hugged her, said, '*Ma'al-salama*, Rabi. I am praying that your firstborn will be a son.'

'I…' Her breath caught in her throat and by the time she had recovered Safia was gone.

Her final visitor was the Emira.

'I had hoped that you would be staying with us for a while, Rabi,' she said. 'The Emir wanted to give you this himself but he has meetings all day.'

She opened the small leather-covered box she was holding to reveal a small falcon, wings spread, delicately modelled in fine gold and suspended from a dark red ribbon.

'It is the Order of the Golden Falcon,' she explained, taking it from the box and fastening it to the lapel of her jacket. 'It has never before been given to a woman but you saved the life of his firstborn son and when he announced the award at the *majlis* this morning I am told that everyone stood and clapped.'

Ruby had known this day would be hard, but now, as Bram's mother kissed both her cheeks, she was struggling to blink back tears that she could not allow to fall.

'I am deeply honoured, my lady. Please thank

the Emir for me.' She forced a smile to her face. 'Will he restore Ibrahim to the throne?'

'He offered it. His brother pressed him to accept.'

'But he refused.'

The Emira smiled. 'You understand him so well.'

Yes.

She understood him. Understood that the love he held in his heart for the woman he had set free to marry his brother was enduring, everlasting. Understood why marriage to her sister would have been unendurable.

'Bram told me that he was born for another age.'

'Maybe.' She sighed. 'He always found it hard to be inside. Was always escaping, looking for adventure.'

'He told me that too. He took me to the blacksmith's shop where he used to play truant as a boy. His friend's son brought me tea.' She picked up her phone to show her the photograph she'd taken of the boy. Instead she found herself looking at the kiss she and Bram had shared at their wedding and reached blindly for the night table, afraid that she was going to faint.

The Emira took the phone from her, looked at the photograph for a long moment, handing it back as Noor appeared in the doorway.

'The car is here, Ruby.'

'Yes.' She hugged the Emira. 'Thank you for your kindness. Please give the Emir my very best wishes.'

'You go with our hearts, Rabi.'

CHAPTER NINE

RUBY HAD EXPECTED her flat, unused for nearly two weeks in a reluctant spring, to be dusty and cold, but it was warm, aired and gleaming. The fridge had been stocked and, beside a pile of post, there was a basket of fruit on the sofa table.

She would have assumed it was Amanda's handiwork but for the fact that there were also half a dozen of the latest bestsellers in hardback, a florist's arrangement of spring flowers and a large box of liquorice allsorts on top of the bookshelf.

Amanda would have bought paperbacks, filled a jug with daffodils picked from her own garden and she didn't know about her love of liquorice allsorts.

A card listing appointments with a physiotherapist at the London Clinic was the clincher.

'You must go to bed now, Ruby,' Noor said. 'I will bring you tea, unpack your clothes, then I will go downstairs. If you need me just call.'

'Downstairs?'

'Bram said your flat is too small for me so I am staying in the one downstairs.'

'Downstairs?' She knew the tenants had been looking for something bigger. They must have moved out while she was away. 'Bram has rented the flat downstairs for you?'

'So that I can be close to look after you.' She took an envelope from her pocket. 'The driver gave me the keys.'

'Right.'

It did explain why Bram hadn't insisted she stay in his London house. This way he could be seen to be taking care of her while she was still, officially, his wife, while keeping her at a distance.

It was the solution she would have come up with if she'd still been his PA and he'd asked her to sort it out.

'Will you be all right on your own in a strange apartment?' she asked.

Noor grinned. 'It will be the first time I've ever had my own home,' she said. 'And I have family. My cousin works in London for the airline owned by Sheikh Zahir. He is Bram's cousin.'

'Yes.' She'd casually spouted that piece of information when she was attempting to impress him.

'We are going to have afternoon tea, visit Borough Market on Sunday morning and go for a ride on the London Eye. Not like you did with Bram when he booked a night-time ride just for the two of you, with all the lights of London at your feet.' She sighed. 'So romantic.'

'Oh.' Her sightseeing trips were culled from

the legend she and Bram had invented, that she had shared with Violet and Leila while Noor had been ironing and stitching and fetching tea.

The Eye had been one of Bram's suggestions and yes, he had made it sound so romantic that she could have fallen in love with him just listening to him.

'I'm not sure about a picnic on the beach,' Noor said with a shiver. 'It's very cold to eat outside.'

'You have to wrap up warm, take a flask of hot soup…' That had been one of her ideas. She'd imagined a winter picnic on a deserted beach, a driftwood fire and the two of them cuddled up close under a tartan blanket sipping hot tomato soup.

She shivered.

'You are cold,' Noor said anxiously.

'I'll be fine once I'm in bed.'

'I will help you.'

'No.' She wanted to be on her own. 'I'll manage.' The sooner she got back to normal, got back to work, the better. 'And don't worry about tea. Just go and sort yourself out. Take anything you need from here.' Although, no doubt, her fridge had been stocked as well.

Her shoulder ached with the effort of getting out of her clothes but a bed had been made up for her on the plane and she'd slept most of the way.

She picked up the mail and curled against the

pillows. Once she'd discarded the junk there wasn't much. Her bank statement, which she put to one side to check later, a bulky envelope from her lawyer and several letters from the bank used by the Queen and addressed to Princess Rabi al-Dance.

The first was from her personal account manager welcoming her to the bank, hoping to meet her when she called in at the branch and to call him for assistance at any time.

The second contained a bank card.

The third a pin number.

The fourth was a statement showing the six-figure balance in her account.

'No…'

She tore open the envelope from her lawyer. It contained a photocopy of the English translation of the contract that Bram had signed and documents requiring her signature regarding the purchase, in her name, of the house where she rented a flat. The accompanying letter congratulated her on her marriage and a suggestion that she make an appointment to discuss making a new will. There was also the contact details of a surveyor who had been engaged to look at the property and organise any necessary repairs. It also confirmed that the last restitution of funds stolen by her father had been made on the day of her wedding.

She quickly scanned the contract, her mouth

drying as she read the terms of the dowry Bram had agreed with Fayad. A house of her own, the jewels, a car, clothes, a maid, driver, annual allowances for wardrobe, personal spending, maintenance of her property, all rising with inflation.

Not a problem. The marriage was over… Except that the divorce settlement terms were the same. A house of her own, maintained in good order, all the jewels she had been given during the marriage and, until she remarried, a maid, driver and all annual allowances.

It went on, laying out what would happen to any children of the marriage, even down to the dowries he would provide for their daughters.

A tear fell on the document. Not for the things she could never accept, but for the children they would never have. For the baby that, but for the deranged act of Ahmed Khadri, she might even now have been carrying.

Not just sex…

She curled her fingers into her palm, feeling the diamond ring that Bram had placed on her finger. She should take it off now, put it away.

Tomorrow. She'd do that tomorrow. And then she'd call Bram and tell him to stop all this nonsense.

Ruby was woken by her phone. She opened her eyes and for a moment had no idea where she was. Then she saw the discoloured patch in the corner of the ceiling, the one she had been all set to paint when she'd had an urgent summons from Amanda to fly to Ras al Kawi.

She was back in her little flat in Camden. The noise she could hear was the swish of wet tyres as the traffic built up to the rush hour frenzy. If she opened her window she would smell wet pavements and diesel fumes instead of the salt tang of the sea.

The phone stopped ringing just as she reached for it. She checked the time, pulled a face but hauled herself out of bed and, having splashed her face with cold water and brushed her teeth, padded barefoot through to the kitchen. While the kettle boiled she checked her voicemail messages.

'Just checking to make sure you had a good flight…' Her hand shook as Bram's soft voice murmured in her ear, so close that she could almost touch him, almost smell him. Had he been waiting for her to ring? Reassure him? 'I'll talk to you later.'

'Yes.'

Realising that she had answered him as if he could hear, she quickly clicked onto the next message.

'Good morning, Ruby.' Amanda's voice, crisp and businesslike, was the dose of smelling salts that she needed. 'Have you seen this morning's paper?' Actually, forget smelling salts; that was more like brimstone. 'Under the circumstances, that seems unlikely,' she continued, 'but I suggest you check out the headlines online then give me a call and let me know what on earth is going on.'

Lori…

No. If it had been Lori, Amanda would have been concerned, sympathetic…

She fumbled with the phone, frantically keying her name into the search engine. The headline that came up was not the one she'd feared.

NEW RULER IN UMM AL BASR

Sheikh Hamad al-Ansari was today installed as the new Emir of Umm al Basr. His father, Sheikh Tariq, who underwent heart surgery last year, is stepping down to allow a younger, more vigorous generation to steer his country into the future.

His oldest son, former international ski champion Sheikh Ibrahim al-Ansari, was disinherited five years ago after a drunken incident in a London fountain and although he and his new English wife, Princess Rabi al-Dance, were at Sheikh Tariq's birthday celebrations earlier this month, a palace spokesman confirmed that, while he will support his brother in every way, he will con-

tinue to concentrate on his private business interests.

There was a small formal head-shot of the new Ruler at the top of the piece, but beneath it were two more photographs. One was that horrible picture of Bram throwing his heritage away in a London fountain so that the woman he loved could marry his brother. The other was of herself in a shimmering dress, diamonds and rubies at her throat, her desert prince at her side.

She was still staring at it when there was a ring at the doorbell. She opened it without looking up, assuming that it was Noor, come to check up on her. Already hitting fast-dial to call Amanda.

'I'll have to find you the spare key,' she said, stepping back.

'That's a good start.'

In her ear Amanda was saying, 'That was quick, considering you're apparently on your honeymoon.'

'I'll call you back,' she said, disconnecting. 'Bram.'

She had been so sure that she'd never see him again that she barely stopped herself from putting out a hand to make sure that he was real. But an illusion had no scent and his, so familiar, was overlaid with that of coffee and warm pastry. 'What are you doing here?'

'Bringing my wife breakfast.' He was carrying a bag from an upmarket bakery. 'Coffee and warm *pain au chocolat*,' he said.

'How—?'

'The sitting room is on the right?' He removed a soft goatskin bomber jacket that was spotted with raindrops and then sat down on the sofa.

'What is this, Bram?' she demanded, although it was hard to stand on her dignity in a T-shirt nightie that was never going to pass the 'princess' test. She should go and put on a wrap, slippers…

'I am catching up, *ya habibati*.' He smiled up at her. 'Is that supposed to be a hedgehog?'

Beloved? He loved Safia…

'It is a hedgehog,' she said, perching on the edge of the sofa, leaving the maximum space between them, pulling the nightshirt over her knees. 'It's Mrs Tiggy-Winkle.' His grin was unnerving her. 'She's a very industrious hedgehog. And kind.'

'Then she is the perfect choice for you.' He took a carton from the bag and offered it to her.

'I'll pour them into mugs,' she said, putting it back in the bag and jumping up. 'And put the pastries on plates or they'll make a terrible mess.'

She hung on the counter for a long moment, wanting him so much but knowing that every moment he was with her Safia would be in his heart, his thoughts.

She jumped as he reached over her head to unhook a couple of mugs, poured the coffee into them.

'I don't understand why you're here,' she said, unwrapping the pastries, sliding them onto a plate, knowing that she could never eat them.

'Don't you?'

His breath was warm against the nape of her neck. All she had to do was lean back and he would have his arms around her. She picked up the coffee, turned and found herself confronted by his soft sweater. Wanting to lean into it, feel the softness against her cheek, feel his heartbeat.

She swallowed. 'No.'

'First we married, then we fell in love and now we are going to have the courtship. As I recall, this is how our story begins. I call on you at sunrise with coffee and *pain au chocolat*—'

'It's raining.'

He took the cups from her, put them on the counter, took her face between his hands.

'Beyond the clouds the sun is shining, Ruby, and this is just the beginning. Tomorrow the rain will stop and we might go to Kew Gardens, or take a boat down to Hampton Court, or have lunch in a little restaurant I know right on the bridge at Windsor.'

'Bram…' she protested.

'When you are stronger we will have our picnic on a beach, we will ride on the Downs, and in the winter we will go to Switzerland and make snowmen—'

'Stop!' He was offering her everything she wanted—a life with him—but she knew… 'I know,' she said. 'I know everything.'

'What do you know, Ruby?'

'That you love Safia. You gave up everything for her and would have done it again for Bibi. All she had to do was ask. A man would only do that for someone he loved, Bram. That's why you dropped out, became a recluse. She broke your heart.'

'Is that why you ran away?'

'I didn't run,' she said. Then, because she couldn't lie to him, 'I flew.'

He ran his fingers through her hair, pushing the curls back from her face as if to make her see him more clearly. 'My marriage to Safia was arranged when we were children, Ruby. I loved her because she was to be my wife, but not in the way you think of love. Not in the way I love you. It was duty, honour.'

'For family and state.'

'For family and state,' he agreed. 'If I'd loved her the way I love you, I would not have kept putting it off while I followed the ski circuit. I could not have waited…' He drew her close, put his arms around her. 'What haunted me, what I will never forget, my darling girl, is that if I had not seen the look that passed between them I would never have known that every time she lay with me there would have been a part of her heart that longed for another man. For his children.'

'But that's…' She stopped.

'That's what you thought it would be like if you stayed with me? That I would make love to you with another woman in my heart?'

'Are you saying that's why you would not marry Bibi?' she said. 'Because you knew her heart would be somewhere else?'

'That, and the fact that she was too young, a pawn to her father's ambitions, and I have to admit the thought that she would rather be cutting up cadavers in a laboratory than providing Umm al Basr with an heir did leave me a little underwhelmed.' He caught her chin, tilted her face so that she was looking up at him. 'Was that a smile?'

'Very nearly,' she admitted.

'Shall we sit down and have the coffee and pastries before they get cold?' he suggested. 'Then we can plan how this courtship will go.'

'If we stick to the script we should be in bed,' she pointed out.

'I have flown here overnight on a scheduled flight so bed does sound very attractive right now but if you only want me for my body… Oh, a smile and a blush.'

'You knew.'

'If "just sex" would do it for you, you wouldn't have spent the last few years alone, my love.'

'No.' He waited. 'What had Safia been praying for, Bram?'

'For me to find love, as she and Hamad found it.'

'You said her prayers had been answered.'

'I found you, Ruby.'

'And let me go.'

'Only so that we could start again. At the beginning. Make our legend real.'

'In my beginning,' she said, lifting her hands to his face, sliding her fingers through his hair, 'we forgot the coffee and began.'

* * * * *

SPECIAL EXCERPT FROM

HARLEQUIN® Romance

Pastry chef Gemma Rizzo never expected to see Vincenzo Gagliardi again. And now he's not just the duke who left her brokenhearted...he's her new boss!

RETURN OF HER ITALIAN DUKE,
the first book in **The Billionaire's Club** *trilogy*
by Rebecca Winters.

Read on for a sneak preview:

Since he'd returned to Italy, thoughts of Gemma had come back full force. At times he'd been so preoccupied, the guys were probably ready to give up on him. To think that after all this time and searching for her, she was right here. Bracing himself, he took the few steps necessary to reach Takis's office.

With the door ajar he could see a polished-looking woman in a blue-and-white suit with dark honey-blond hair falling to her shoulders. She stood near the desk with her head bowed, so he couldn't yet see her profile.

Vincenzo swallowed hard to realize Gemma was no longer the teenager with short hair he used to spot when she came bounding up the stone steps of the *castello* from school wearing her uniform. She'd grown into a curvaceous woman.

"Gemma." He said her name, but it came out gravelly.

A sharp intake of breath reverberated in the office. She wheeled around. Those unforgettable brilliant green eyes with the darker green rims fastened on him. A stillness seemed to surround her. She grabbed hold of the desk.

"Vincenzo… I—I think I must be hallucinating."

"I'm in the same condition." His gaze fell on the lips he'd kissed that unforgettable night. Their shape hadn't changed, nor the lovely mold of her facial features.

She appeared to have trouble catching her breath. "What's going on? I don't understand."

"Please sit down and I'll tell you."

He could see she was trembling. When she didn't do his bidding, he said, "I have a better idea. Let's go for a ride in my car. It's parked out front. We'll drive to the lake at the back of the estate, where no one will bother us. Maybe by the time we reach it, your shock will have worn off enough to talk to me."

Hectic color spilled into her cheeks. "Surely you're joking. After ten years of silence, you suddenly show up here this morning, honestly thinking I would go anywhere with you?"

Make sure to read…
RETURN OF HER ITALIAN DUKE by Rebecca Winters, available March 2017 wherever Harlequin® Romance books and ebooks are sold.

www.Harlequin.com

HREXP0217